THE MOLECULE MEN

THE MOLECULE MEN

by

SIR FRED HOYLE

and

GEOFFREY HOYLE

HARPER & ROW, PUBLISHERS
New York, Evanston, San Francisco, London

First published in England under the title *The Molecule Men and the Monster of Loch Ness*

STANDARD BOOK NUMBER: 06-011974-8

LIBRARY OF CONGRESS CATALOG CARD NUMBER: 74-184380

To J.B. and Jacquetta

THE MOLECULE MEN

LUNAR DUST

I watched with impatience as luggage emerged from a kind of crematorium in reverse. Fortunately, I thought sourly, this labour-saving airport device was only half automatic. Recently I'd encountered a fully automated system, a marvel of technology, which ripped labels off outgoing luggage and accumulated incoming bags in mysterious undiscoverable back-waters.

My profession has two sides to it. On the surface I'm a Cambridge don. Under the surface I'm what you might call an industrial spy, nothing political or military. Oddly enough, the two activities fit very well together, the respectable side being a natural complement for the not-so-respectable. While in Cambridge I work on highly academic problems and this gains me access to chemical companies all over the world. It gives me the status to walk in at the front door, so to speak. And out by the front door too, having learned one or two things that my company, United Chemicals, wants to know.

On this particular morning I was irritated and sour because I'd been sent to the United States on a wild goose chase. The lunar soil episode started when NASA reported that plants grow more rapidly in it than in ordinary terrestrial soil. Why?

On account of some trace element, fairly obviously. Plant growth depends not just on the common constituents of soil but on small quantities of rare materials as well. Since the rare materials are different on the Moon, it was a fair bet that the root of the problem lay there. United Chemicals was interested because of the possibility of introducing the same critical trace materials into ordinary agriculture, as a kind of super fertilizer. My doubt, the reason for my lack of enthusiasm, was simply that the odds were a hundred-to-one against the idea being economically feasible.

I was turning over in my mind certain pungent remarks specially selected for one of the Directors of United Chemicals, when an incident occurred that brightened the day for me. After collecting my bag at wearisome length I was walking unobtrusively through the customs hall when I was knocked sideways by a man in a harsh blue suit and a Homburg hat. As I retrieved my case a posse of officials rushed past in pursuit of the now rapidly retreating figure. What an incredible amateur I thought to myself.

But as soon as I stepped outside the airport building, at about 7.30 a.m. on a cold dark January morning, I realized the fellow had a fair chance of slipping away in the misty gloom.

The wind was chilly, so instantly I jumped into the nearest taxi, saying 'United Chemicals, in the Strand.'

On the motorway the taxi pulled laboriously into the right-hand lane to overtake an airline bus. As we moved alongside I glanced idly up at the windows. A hard flat face was looking down at me. It wasn't the face itself that had particular meaning, it was the electric blue suit the fellow was wearing. All the way to the Strand I kept wondering why anybody would wear a suit like that, especially if he were making a break for it.

CHAPTER TWO

IN VINO VERITAS

Cambridge is the most depressing place on wintry days. The east wind slices across the open fenland turning the portals of learning into cold icy stone. In fact the weather conditions are very similar to the feelings that run like hidden rivers under the placid exterior of the city.

My college is Emmanuel, but the events I am now to describe took place in Jesus. A fellow chemist had invited me there to the annual Candlemas Feast, which took place about a week after my return from the United States, in the first few days of February.

I suppose seventy-five people were at dinner, all men. We sat ourselves down at long tables, with candlelight shedding those ominous long fluttering shadows. Gradually as more and more wine was consumed the sound level rose higher and higher until at last we were all bawling our heads off. My host, Carswell, a rubicund, jolly-looking man, who I happened to know had a connection with Government Intelligence, insisted towards the end of the meal that we should go back to his rooms—with a few others—for a final nightcap.

We were about to leave the Dining Hall when I noticed an elderly Fellow with flowing white hair attacking a fly on the table in front of him. With furious persistence the old man flailed away with his napkin, but the insect just seemed to hop from side to side, somehow avoiding the napkin and the wind it produced. Then in apparent desperation the old boy let loose with the flat of his hand on the middle of the table.

'Tremendous reactions, old Simons has,' said Carswell, rising.

'He's pretty strong certainly,' I replied as the crockery settled back onto the table. The old man drew back his hand but there was no sign of a crushed fly underneath. I smiled and followed Carswell out of the Hall.

'I've seen him around, in summer.'

'Pruning the bushes no doubt.'

'I suppose he's retired.'

'Officially, yes. Unofficially he's still writing the second volume of his history of England. Been at it for thirty years.'

'What happened to the first volume?'

'A best-seller to have lasted so long,' said Carswell as we entered his rooms. 'Gentlemen, may I introduce Dr John West.'

I nodded to three men already assembled there.

'Here we have another historian, Chris Spottiswood,' went on my host, pointing to a lean fellow who looked like Chalky in a Giles cartoon.

'This is the Dean, Professor Underwood, and this is Mr Harrison, from London.'

'Good evening, Dr West,' said Harrison, standing up to address me. He was a tall thin man, dressed very precisely, dinner jacket and old-fashioned stiff shirt.

'Well now, who's for port?' asked Carswell, clinking glasses.

We sat digesting our meal and making polite conversation for a while. The talk among such a small number was coherent rather than scattered. Eventually it emerged that Harrison was a police officer, Special Branch. I say 'eventually', for I could have told them so from the moment I set eyes on the man. At any rate I could have pinpointed him as something special, whether police, intelligence service, or the like. In my not-so-respectable capacity, I've seen these types so often before.

While Harrison was entertaining the group with one or two prepared anecdotes, I turned the situation over in my mind. So far as I was concerned there was nothing in it for the police. The only sensitive area would lie with the investigating officers at the Treasury. And this would be more a matter for United Chemicals generally than for me in particular.

The point of course is that you can't finance espionage, whether through government or through industry, in a manner suited to a normal balance sheet. Every government agency has its own special budget which lies beyond normal scrutiny. Industrially we are not permitted special budgets, at any rate officially. So rules simply have to be broken. The situation is absurd but it goes on.

Eventually the party broke up, not before time. Harrison contrived to delay me a moment while Carswell was seeing the others out.

'Dr West, I believe you travelled on TWA Flight 99 from Chicago? On the night of January 23rd.'

Deliberately I took out my diary and flipped through the pages.

'That's right. I flew from Chicago on the 23rd, TWA. I'm not sure about the flight number.'

'What time did you land?'

'I suppose about 7.15 a.m.'

'That would be the right flight.'

With rising anger I noted that Carswell hadn't rejoined us. Planting Harrison on me had been deliberate then.

'Inspector Harrison, if you have questions to ask me—official questions—why not arrange an appointment?'

Rather to my surprise Harrison seemed embarrassed. He scratched his ear for a moment.

'Well, to be absolutely frank, I don't have *official* questions. It's just that I'm badly puzzled.'

'By what?'

'A man in a Homburg hat.'

I must have reacted, for Harrison picked up my reflex.

'You saw him?' he asked.

'Saw him! He almost bowled me over. Ran into me in the customs area.'

'Then you could describe him?'

'As a matter of fact I couldn't. By the time I'd recovered my wits he was away, disappearing into the distance. Oddly enough it was the hat and the colour of his suit which occupied my attention.'

'Blue?'

'Very blue.'

'Surely you have some impression of the man?'

'Well, I'm pretty certain he was of compact build. Not small—but chunky.'

9

'Did you notice him on the plane?'

'No.'

'In the queue at the immigration desk?'

'No.'

'Can you describe what happened after the plane landed. Up to the time of the incident in the customs hall.'

'It was quite a walk from the arrival gate to immigration. I put on a fair turn of speed, partly to stretch my legs and partly to be at the head of the immigration queue. I passed perhaps a dozen people. Your man wasn't among them. The immigration people led me straight through. Then I waited quite a time for my bag.'

'Did you see the man—while you were waiting?'

'No.'

'After you got your bag, exactly what happened?'

'Well, there are two exits, one marked: FOR PASS-ENGERS WITH GOODS TO DECLARE—or some such title, and the other for passengers without goods to declare. I went through the second. The collision happened shortly after that.'

'I see. Was it a random encounter?'

'Meaning what, Inspector?'

'You didn't see him again, this man?'

'No.'

Which wasn't true. I was pretty sure I'd seen the fellow again on the airline bus. I didn't feel like admitting it because it seemed too much of a coincidence. The last thing I wanted was to have Harrison connecting me with the Homburg hat.

'What was the fellow up to?' I asked.

'I wish I knew.'

'You must know something. Otherwise you wouldn't have arranged with Carswell . . .'

'I'm sorry about that.'

Harrison was scratching his head now. He certainly looked a seriously baffled man.

'It started at the immigration desk. One of the immigration officers became suspicious.'

'About what?'

'Just about the man.'

'His passport?'

'No, the passport seemed in order.'

'I don't understand.'

Harrison paused for quite a while, and then went on, 'I'm not sure I do either. When I questioned the officer he insisted the man *didn't seem right*. Those were his words.'

Oddly enough, I had a similar feeling.

'He left his fellow officer—there were two officers on the desk?' asked Harrison.

'Yes. As far as my experience goes there always are.'

'Well, he left his fellow officer to watch the man while he went to get the TWA passenger list.'

'I'd expect immigration officers to have the passenger list already.'

'Apparently they hadn't.'

'Then what happened?'

'Very simple. The man made a break for it. He ran down into the customs area where he collided with you, and then out into the open.'

'It was pretty foggy and dark outside.'

'The airport security people were plain slack, if you ask me.'

'Why are you so concerned with the case, Inspector?'

Harrison shifted his legs uneasily, sweeping them over a wide arc. In the rather dim light of Carswell's rooms I noticed his hair was beginning to silver. 'Why shouldn't I be concerned with it?' he answered.

'Come off it, Inspector. The Special Branch isn't called in to chase every immigrant-on-the-loose. There has to be a lot more to it.'

'Which I might prefer to keep to myself.'

'Of course. But since you were at such pains to make this a social conversation I thought I might ask. You must have followed up the passport. What was the name?'

'Adcock. R.A.Adcock.'

'I suppose it was forged?'

'Yes and no. The material of the passport was genuine—the paper. But no passport was issued to any R.A.Adcock on the date stamped on it.'

'By the Foreign Office?'

'Nothing by the Foreign Office.'

'So the forger had access to the official water-mark. You'd better start watching for counterfeit banknotes.'

'The point hadn't escaped me.'

'And the address—on the passport?'

'Nineteen Wellington Road, Pimlico.'

'Where dwells a little old lady, no doubt.'

'Where dwells a rough tough dock worker. Talk to him about Homburg hats and he'd give you a quick left that might send you to casualty.'

'I still don't see what there is in all this to involve you personally, Inspector. Or me either.'

'You're hardly seeking to tell me my own business, Dr West?'

'Of course not. But I take it you're checking up on all available passengers—on this flight I mean?'

'As far as I can.'

'A lot of trouble for a straightforward case.'

'A straightforward case of what?'

'Forgery and smuggling.'

'Not straightforward.' Harrison leaned forward and tapped me on the knee. 'Let me tell you this. The name of the docker is Ronald Arthur Adcock. No doubt about it. I've checked him from A to Z. What manner of forger would use an actual name and an actual address? Besides there was no Adcock on the TWA passenger list.'

For the first time I began to realize that Harrison had a genuine sense of unease. So had I myself for that matter. It just didn't figure, as the Americans would say, any of it. Both Harrison and I, in different ways, were concerned with unusual aspects of life. On the face of it we might have been expected to react to unusual circumstances more calmly than most people. But this affair was so far outside our experience, it verged so much on the ridiculous, as to put us quite out of stride. Farce doesn't mix with cloak and dagger stuff. Harrison put it very well, just before Carswell returned.

'I've always believed there was a clear-cut logical explanation to everything. This business reached my desk by way of information, not for action. But I just couldn't put it out of my mind. So I simply had to get involved. There has to be an explanation somewhere.'

It was dark, the main College lights being turned off, as Carswell let me out of the Jesus car park. Since he was unaware that I knew a good deal about his extra-curricular activities, I gave no hint that the connection with Harrison had been obvious to me. I drove to my home in Newnham feeling all the time there was some-one immediately behind me. Not since I was a small boy had I felt so frightened, particularly at the moment I entered the darkened house.

CHAPTER THREE

THE LAW LENDS A HAND

The weeks rolled by with the usual outrages continually reported in the press. Turmoil abroad, strikes at home, demonstrations against this and that, tragic accidents, and the usual crop of violent crimes.

A bank robbery in Lewisham was exceptional only in that it was perpetrated not by masked intruders equipped with guns and smoke bombs but by one of the bank's own tellers. The case gathered interest, however, when it came before the magistrates' court. The defendant, a 'quiet man' of about forty-five with a hitherto blameless record, proceeded to deny the charge with the utmost vehemence. He continued to do so throughout his subsequent trial saying he had not gone to work at all on the day in question. But when asked for evidence of some sort of alibi he could produce none. And to the question of where he'd been on the fateful day all he could answer was 'my mind was a blank'. Against a mountain of eye-witness accounts of the robbery, some witnesses being his own colleagues at the bank—men he'd worked with for several years—this flimsy defence stood no chance of success. The bewildered teller was given a seven-year sentence, and nothing further would have been heard of him, at any rate for the period of his sentence, had it not been for a remarkable intervention from R. A. Adcock.

The morning paper carried half a column:

ROW FLARES OVER MISIDENTIFICATION

A man, charged yesterday at Lewisham police station in the name of Ronald Arthur Adcock, 41, of 19 Wellington Road, Pimlico, confessed to the robbery of the National Westminster Bank, Lewisham, High Street on February 23rd. He will appear in court on Friday.

In April, Kenneth Sheppard, a teller at the bank, was tried and convicted for this robbery. At his trial Sheppard strenuously denied all knowledge of the crime and collapsed when sentenced to seven years' imprisonment.

Disquiet is being widely expressed at what may be yet another case of misidentification. Sir William Birch, Conservative M.P. for Streatham, said: 'There have been too many serious mistakes of this kind. Coming on top of two misidentification incidents in Bradford and the recent one in Glasgow makes me feel that we are all in jeopardy if this sort of thing is allowed to go on. I shall be asking the Home Secretary for a full statement on the case.'

Friday the 23rd found me early at the Civic Hall, Lewisham.

'Good morning, can you tell me where I can find the Magistrates' Court?' I asked at the information desk.

'Two floors up. Then it's number 4, last door on the left.'

I suppose the courtroom was something of the order of seventy by fifty feet. The public benches were already reasonably full. I managed to squeeze into the front one. Surveying the scene, to my right was the prisoner's dock with a staircase leading down to the cells. In the middle of the room, an odd assortment of people were distributed around a large square table, some facing a kind of stage with a long narrow table and three large magisterial chairs on it, others with their backs to the stage. Behind the official chairs and table were two enormous windows which let in a certain amount of sunlight on an otherwise drab décor.

I looked around at the public benches to see what my fellow spectators were like. I wondered whether they were perhaps friends of Sheppard, or just men and women with a curiously morbid attitude—like the people who stand by the roadside watching victims being removed from an automobile accident. Continuing my survey I realized that on the far right beyond the prisoner's dock were still more people. From the amount of paper they had in front of them I decided they must be journalists. Nobody seemed concerned about the severity of the place. In an aisle near the main door two policewomen were swapping jokes with a policeman. Officials hurried backwards and forwards using much energy but apparently achieving little.

I suppose a court of law is one of the few places, perhaps the only place, where you can simply go in and take a seat without a single eyebrow being raised. It seems that here at least everybody looks rigorously after his or her own business. And the court itself is perhaps flattered by your presence and is happy to have you there, provided you keep quiet, which is fair enough considering you are consuming light and heat at the taxpayers' expense.

At around ten-thirty, the magistrates, two men and a woman in an extraordinary red hat, walked onto the stage at the far end of the room. The people in the well of the court rose and we were in business.

After dealing with extensions of drinking licences at various public houses and hotels, a whole crop of minor motoring offences came up. The world's finest comic would have been at pains to work any humour into this deadly boring material. The more I heard of it the more I grieved for the magistrates. Listening every day to such stuff would be just about my idea of hell. As each case came and went the public benches emptied a bit, until about midday, when the room began to refill.

Harrison appeared unobtrusively around 11.50. I was surprised that he, like me, took a seat among the 'public'. So he wasn't concerned officially, on the surface anyway. I saw him as he came through the door on the far side of the room, and thereafter I made a conscious effort not to stare in his direction. I expected him to notice me but I had no wish to advertise myself in case he didn't.

R. A. Adcock was at last brought in. The simplest and most graphic way I can describe him is to say that he looked like the fellows who organize Russian peace missions. There was the same square solid build of body, and the same vacancy of face. His hair was clipped short, which emphasized the blunt indistinct features. Undoubtedly the most striking visual impact of the man was again his violent blue suit.

The prosecution read out the charge against the defendant and the clerk of the court informed Adcock of his rights. The man just stared up from the dock at the three magistrates. The clerk then asked Adcock for his name, age and address. Again no response. The clerk and one of the male magistrates, whom I took to be the Chairman, conferred for a few moments. Then the prisoner was brought forward into the witness-box and the same questions were repeated. Adcock appeared to hear them but no answer came.

'Sir, may I ask the defendant a question?' asked the prosecuting council.

A moment was spent while the Chairman again conferred with his clerk. At length an affirmative answer was given.

'Is your name Ronald Arthur Adcock?' asked counsel.

To this question Adcock replied with an enormous cough.

'Is your name Ronald Arthur Adcock?' came the same question again.

Another cough.

'Please answer the question,' said the lady magistrate in a high tone.

'Yes,' replied Adcock with a croak, not unlike a cough.

'Your age?'

Adcock started by showing his hands and then sticking up his fingers to indicate his age.

'Forty-one?' asked the clerk.

Another cough, followed by an eventual 'yes'.

'And your address is 19 Wellington Road, London, S.W.1?'

A whole series of coughs followed, then a gulp which sounded like 'no'.

'You don't live at 19 Wellington Road, London, S.W.1?' asked the Chairman.

Adcock grimaced and shook his head. A confused pause followed with the clerk, magistrates and prosecuting council hurriedly studying their various papers.

'In your confession to the police you stated that you were domiciled at 19 Wellington Road, London, S.W.1. Are you domiciled there or are you not?' demanded the prosecuting counsel in a braying tone well-matched to Adcock's cough. Adcock studied the man carefully and at length. Then just as the Chairman was about to intervene again, he said very slowly and deliberately, 'I am not domiciled.'

'Ah, let me put it this way. Do you live at 19 Wellington Road, London, S.W.1?' asked the clerk.

Long loud coughing from Adcock which the Chairman and counsel after further deliberation were glad to take as an affirmative.

It can well be imagined how at this rate the merest preliminaries took until lunchtime. There was none of the usual business of the prisoner being remanded after a mere three minutes' appearance in court. Adcock somehow managed to exact a terrible toll from his inquisitors. They were now only too glad to call 'time' and retreat to lunch.

I'd hoped to avoid Harrison but he was waiting for me out in the corridor.

20

'Ah, Dr West, I saw you in there. Perhaps you'd care for a bite of lunch.'

'That's very kind of you.'

I saw no point in refusing. In any case a few points had occurred to me which Harrison might be able to clear up. Instead of going out to a local pub he took me down flights of stairs to a police canteen. There were several groups of people, some in uniform, others in civvies. Harrison made no attempt to join any of them but went off to collect cheese, bread and tea for the two of us.

'So that's Adcock.'

'He's an Adcock all right but God only knows who he really is,' grunted Harrison, cutting a large hunk of cheese.

'Do both men live at this address down in Pimlico? Adcock and the docker?'

'Seems like it, but none of my men has seen this Adcock go in or out of the place.'

Harrison swept his feet in my direction, nearly upsetting the cups of liquid on the table. I guessed him to be in his early forties, a few years older than myself.

'So this is the Homburg hat.'

'Mm,' nodded my companion, his mouth full of cheese.

'I can see now why the immigration chap must have been worried. There's something distinctly queer about him.'

'Distinctly.'

'One thing I can't see. This bank robbery business. Adcock just couldn't have been mistaken for that bank teller.'

'Sheppard, no,' came the perfunctory answer.

'Well, why are the police bringing this case?'

'What's your interest, Dr West?' said Harrison, eyeing me.

'Curiosity, I suppose. You started it, the night in Carswell's rooms.'

'Fair enough.'

'That doesn't answer my question.'

'Adcock produced the stolen money.'

'Sheppard didn't have it?'

'None was ever found—nothing connected with Sheppard. Which was why Sheppard managed to make out some sort of defence at his trial.'

'I see. Or rather I don't see, about the identification I mean.'

'It must have been Sheppard who actually took the money.'

'And Adcock was a kind of receiver. His part could have been to get the cash out of the country,' I said without conviction.

'He doesn't look a likely starter, does he?'

I had to admit this fellow in the electric blue suit didn't look to be a likely starter at anything. I said as much and added, 'He certainly doesn't look as if he's ever been in a courtroom before.'

'He doesn't look to me as if he's ever been anywhere before,' replied Harrison taking a sip of tea.

I stared straight into Harrison's face, for a long time, and then muttered, 'not been anywhere before'. That just about summed it up. Adcock lacked all normal social responses. It was as if he'd grown from birth to maturity out of contact with human society.

It was this quality that was proving so disturbing in the courtroom. In all our everyday social interchanges we accept a thousand and one little conventions. Without these, normal dealings are impossible. This was the trouble. This had been the problem with the immigration officer at the airport.

We reassembled at 2 p.m. sharp. The smiling faces of the court officers were gone. I had the notion that over lunch the court had decided there was to be no more nonsense. And indeed everything started at a rip-roaring pace. But inevitably Adcock's methods of replying to questions gradually wore down the prosecuting counsel. There seemed to be nothing he could do to elicit a straightforward answer from the defendant. It took the best part of an hour to clear up Adcock's motive in taking money from the bank. His reasoning dumbfounded everybody. He took the money because he needed it. Didn't everyone else take money from a bank? Hopelessly flustered by this simple-minded defence, counsel flopped down in his seat while the clerk tried to straighten the situation out by explaining to the prisoner that one didn't just take money from a bank, unless the money had first been deposited there. To this, Adcock answered with a noise that sounded like the barking of a great animal.

I am sure all three magistrates would dearly have loved to commit Adcock for contempt there and then. So much was obvious from the splutterings erupting from the stage. But it was equally obvious that Adcock wasn't being contemptuous at all. It was rather as if he'd come there, to court, as an observer, just to see what went on, not to be tried for some crime or other.

23

At length they got round to the point that was puzzling me so sorely. How had Adcock taken the money from the bank? Here the prisoner became more animated. His answers were no longer confined to monosyllables. But this didn't help a great deal since the answers were extremely obscure. Adcock had somehow prevented a man who worked at the bank—that would be the un.fortunate Sheppard—from going there, and he himself had gone along to the bank, but in Sheppard's 'shape'. He'd walked in with a small suitcase, filled it with money and walked out. As simple as that. Absolutely nothing to it. Why had he confessed? Here Adcock pointed accusingly up at the three magistrates and said, 'To prevent the "untruth" which they had created.' It was as if the magistrates, sitting up there on the stage, were in dock, not Adcock.

The officials of the court were wilting badly now. Counsel, in tones of despair, made come-back after come-back concerning the 'shape' business. How was it possible to go to a bank in another man's shape? After several wholly incomprehensible replies, Adcock at last lifted up his right arm, like a priest giving the Benediction. The court seemed to go quiet and I had the odd notion Adcock was calling a halt to the proceedings. After three hours or so of this indescribable stuff nobody was in a fit state to do much more than watch.

Suddenly the right arm was back on top of the dock. This gave Adcock the necessary balance and pressure to lift himself bodily on to one of the containing sides. The three policemen with the job of escorting the prisoner hardly moved. A quick leap and Adcock was up there on the magistrates' table. A couple of strides or so and he was on the sill of one of the large windows.

If you or I were asked to walk through a windowpane I wonder how we would go about it. For my part, if I'd plenty of time, I'd kick out the glass and carefully ease myself through once the hole was large enough. If however there were a fire in the room and it was impossible to get out by the door, I'd cover my face with say an arm and move through the window shoulder first. What seemed absolutely incredible was that Adcock, having reached the enormous window, should just walk through it like a silhouette. I saw him begin to fall, down into the street. He made no sound, no scream. I marvelled at the fact that he'd just put all the parts of his body—legs, chest, head and arms straight through the window, all together. The only sound was of tinkling glass followed moments later by shouts from passers-by outside. At this, pandemonium broke loose in the courtroom.

I felt Harrison's body move as he left the bench beside me. Leaping to my feet I half ran into the corridor outside.

'Come on, you two, don't just stand there,' I heard Harrison's raised voice, somewhere up in front of me.

Reaching the head of the staircase, I saw that we were now joined by a couple of policemen. What I hadn't realized before was that the streets, back and front of the building, were on different levels. From the courtroom to the street level at the front the drop was a couple of floors. But Adcock had taken the drop at the back. This was at least three floors. At each turn of

25

the staircase I grabbed hard at the banisters and yanked myself round, almost sliding on the concrete in my leather-soled shoes.

I was last out through the heavy wooden doors. It wasn't a wide street at the back and it had cars parked either side, so there wasn't much more than a car's width down the middle. A small crowd gathered to watch Harrison and his companions run almost aimlessly around, rather like hounds looking for a scent

'Where the hell is he?' Harrison asked as he hurried by.

I shrugged my shoulders and looked up at the broken window of the courtroom. It must have been some fifty-odd feet above the street and yet there was no sign of a broken body.

'I saw it,' said a shaken woman, catching hold of Harrison as he shot by yet again.

'What did you see?'

'I saw this man, falling from up there.'

'What happened when he reached the pavement?'

'I closed my eyes,' came the reply.

'What did you see when you opened them?'

'Nothing on the pavement—or in the road. I thought I'd been seeing things but when I looked up, there was this broken window. But here,' the woman pointed at the ground, 'there wasn't nobody.'

'When you opened your eyes did you see a car driving away?'

'No.'

'My God, look at that!'

Harrison clutched me by the shoulder and pointed

upward towards a dark cloud. We must have missed it at first, I suppose because it was projected against one of the other buildings. It rose and fell as it now proceeded across the face of the courtroom building. It gave the impression of searching for something. Even as we watched, it swept into the courtroom through the shattered window. It was only then that I realized that the dark cloud consisted of bees.

'I don't believe it,' I shouted, 'come on.'

Harrison was right behind me as I started pounding back up all those flights of stairs. Even before I hit the first floor my heart was racing fit to burst. It was an effort to keep my feet from catching the stairs. Harrison swore loudly as he tripped and stumbled just behind me.

Reaching the corridor outside the courtroom I paused to regain some composure while Harrison belted past me and then stopped suddenly. Above the agonized yells from inside we could hear the zz-zz of angry bees. It needed no imagination to know that people were being stung good and proper in there. Suddenly, almost as if a dam wall had broken, the courtroom door burst open and people surged out, white-faced and terrified. A policeman's eyes were red and swelling. A man in a green jacket crept into a corner of the passage sobbing.

The temptation was too great. Leaving Harrison open-mouthed, I shouldered my way to the swing door, 'Get back, you silly bugger,' a voice yelled near my ear. But I pushed into the courtroom.

The sight that greeted me was fantastic. The air was full of enormous black specks silhouetted against the windows at the far end of the room. A violent push sent me falling across one of the benches. I steadied myself and then climbed up to get a better view. On the floor in the well of the courtroom lay a mass of yelling, thrashing humanity. Suddenly a squadron of bees came at me from the direction of the ceiling, flying straight for my face. I ducked only to find another group coming in from behind. This time I was hit firmly by perhaps six or seven enormous, and I mean enormous, bees. My mistake here was to take a swipe at them to clear my face. Inevitably I was stung for my pains. As if all hell was after me I dived for the door. Luck was with me, for I found a reasonably clear path, and was through and outside before another attack hit me. I was shaking and rightly so, for the fear engendered by a whole swarm is vastly greater than the fear of being stung by a single bee. What I found exceedingly frightening was that instead of flying around more or less at random like a normal swarm, this one appeared to be organized, flying in groups apparently directed at particular objectives.

'What the devil did you do that for?' muttered Harrison as I looked at the red swelling on my hand.

'I had to find out.'

'What?'

'What those bees were doing. They must have made a direct line for the magistrates, clerk and prosecuting counsel. Look, Harrison, once you've got the injured people out of there, seal the whole room off,' I said thoughtfully, almost forgetting the pain of the sting.

'Why?' asked Harrison.

'For God's sake, man, don't just stand there asking

why all the time. Seal that outer window. Get some plastic sheet or something and cover it straight away.'

'To keep the bees in?' asked Harrison incredulously.

'Yes, yes, yes!' I almost shouted, wondering how the fellow could be so obtuse. My sense of urgency at last stirred him into action.

I left Harrison giving orders. Ambulance men were appearing now, and several firemen also rushed past me. A policewoman showed me where a first-aid box was kept. Within minutes I had the pain of the sting reduced with some alkali. The policewoman was still there. 'Why should those bees go mad like that?' she asked.

'They probably would have been all right if the swarm had been left alone,' I answered glibly.

'But there's no pollen in the courtroom!'

'They probably swept in automatically—it has been known to happen—bees invading houses.'

'Still seems very strange to me,' she muttered.

I made my way out into the street again. A fireman was cautiously climbing to the top of his ladder when suddenly the swarm came buzzing out of the broken window. Luckily for him it made off over the house-tops on the other side of the street.

I stood reflecting that the might of the law had not been very effective in its dealings with R. A. Adcock.

CHAPTER FOUR

THE ARMED SERVICES INTERVENE

Harrison came storming out of the building, his face as black as thunder.

'There's nothing to be done here,' I said lamely.

'Can't get anything done in this damn dump. It's not the sort of place where anything gets done. Full of people pushing paper around, government forms mostly. The whole bloody building's nothing but one enormous collection of pigeon-holes,' he said in disgust and started walking towards the High Street.

'Better go some place where you can get action.'

'You're damn right, that's where we're going.'

Harrison walked straight out into the road and stopped a cab coming from the opposite direction. In moments he had the two-way traffic halted and the taxi pointing in the direction of London. We had almost reached Westminster Bridge before the flames and smoke vanished from the policeman's face.

'You gave me the idea back there that you'd some notion of what was going on,' he said abruptly, swinging his legs and feet dangerously close to my ankle bones.

'I may have a few ideas,' I said, looking at the solid worry line that ran across the middle of the man's forehead.

'Go on then, I'd like to hear them.'

'No doubt, but I'm not in the mood.'

'Bloody cagey scientists,' growled Harrison, 'never able to get a straight answer out of them.'

'Maybe, but I like to think before I talk.'

'Then think fast. You mightn't be around much longer.'

This remark kept me occupied as the taxi made good time across London considering the time of day. The driver pulled into the kerb opposite what looked like a builder's yard in Lambolle Road near Hampstead Heath. Harrison paid off the cab and we crossed the road and went into the yard through two large wooden gates that made up the entrance. The place was full of piles of wood and steel tubing. Ladders rested against the back of a house and a rusty cement mixer guarded the back door.

'Quite a set up,' I muttered looking at the crumbling plaster.

Harrison slid open a door and we went down a staircase into a large room crammed with electronic equipment.

'Sergeant Hope,' called Harrison.

'Sir,' came the reply from an office off the main gadget room.

'Take care to have a good look around, Dr West. I won't be a moment.'

Harrison strode across the room to the office, where I presumed he wished to confer with the Sergeant.

'Good afternoon,' I said to a young man sitting before a control panel dominated by a large screen.

'Afternoon.'

31

'Radar equipment?' I asked.

'That's your guess.'

Obviously I wasn't going to get any significant information out of the lad, so I turned my attention to the rest of the room. Covering virtually the entire end wall was an enormous electrically operated plotter showing the whole of the British Isles. Bright little pinpoints of light moved to and fro around the London area.

'Helicopters,' said Harrison coming up behind me.

'You mean you're looking for that swarm of bees?'

'You're damn right I'm looking. Telephones were the one useful piece of equipment they had in that god-awful Lewisham place. Look I think we'd better start getting the record straight,' he said handing me a small blue file.

'S.I.9,' I murmured as I flicked through the pages. 'I still don't think I can be of any help.'

'To a certain extent I agree with you, but my superiors seem to think otherwise.'

'They seem to be very sure of themselves, your superiors.'

'Never argue with the powers that be.'

'You might say that. I thought a security clearance was needed, for classified information,' I said as I handed back the blue folder in which so much of my past activities were detailed.

'How long have you had a file on me?' I continued.

'Years,' said Harrison, walking to the far end of the room to watch the plotter.

'Completely automatic?'

'At this end, yes. A computer takes all the information and relates it to positions here on the board. These white dots are helicopters—these blue ones here are fast-moving aircraft.'

'Why are they covering such a large area outside London?' Some blue dots were as far west as Exeter.

'Some sort of service rivalry I would imagine. The helicopters are army and the supersonic stuff is airforce. Look we even have the navy combing the Channel and North Sea.' Harrison pointed to large blobs of yellow light.

I watched the pattern for a while, noting just how quiet it was in this subterranean operations room. Somewhere I felt there had to be a normal straightforward control centre, with the whirl of ever-changing pictures riding on a babel of sound. I can never understand why pilot-to-ground communications are always so loud and of such exceedingly poor quality.

I found myself imagining the telephone calls to every bee keeper in the land, hounding them for information. There might even be a scanning satellite somewhere. Little bee, Big Brother is watching you.

Suddenly Harrison prodded the glass screen with a forefinger. Looking closely I saw a small red speck.

'Get someone in there to find out what that is!' he shouted.

'Unidentified object travelling north-east from Tottenham, can you investigate?' came the voice of the young man at the control panel.

Suddenly the room was filled with static and verbal confusion.

33

'This is Red Dawn calling Sunrise. Unidentified object travelling north-east from Tottenham, can you investigate?'

'Sunrise to Red Dawn, will do.'

More static and then quiet, broken a few moments later by a raucous voice. 'Have visual contact with small dark cloud formation, will investigate.'

'O.K., Sunrise.'

'Sunrise to Red Dawn—unidentified object turns out to be a swarm of bees.'

'I read you, Sunrise.'

'Hellish big size of bee,' crackled the voice a moment later, 'and moving north as though their lives depended on it.'

'Tell that pilot to get out of their way,' I shouted, too late.

'By God, they're dive bombing me from above. They're covering the outside of the ship,' went on the voice now in real alarm.

'This is Red Dawn, get that kite of yours out of there.'

'Red Dawn, this is Sunrise. I can't see, they've damn well covered the windscreen, and they've jammed the screen wiper too. They're enormous bloody great things.'

'I don't understand it,' growled Harrison.

'It won't do,' I said, absorbed with a new thought.

'What won't do?'

'Those bees are too big. They wouldn't live long,' I went on, 'not bees as big as that. They wouldn't be able to absorb enough oxygen.'

'How big are they?'

'From what I saw, I should say the size of a golf ball.'

Harrison gripped me by the arm and took me into the office. A middle-aged man in plain clothes, the redoubtable Sergeant no doubt, got up and left us.

'Now what the devil are you talking about, Dr West? If you know something definite about this business, you'd better start telling me.' Harrison now had a really grey and worried look about him, so rather against my better judgment I decided to speak what was in my mind.

'I only know what I can deduce from the facts,' I said, perching myself on the edge of a desk.

'And that is what?'

'Mainly that a man turned somehow into a swarm of bees.'

'I've been trying desperately to resist that conclusion.'

'Because you think it's impossible?'

'Yes. I know it's impossible,' came the resolute answer.

'Life itself isn't really possible, is it?'

'How's that?'

'Well, we accept life because we're used to it. But if you think about it, abstractly I mean, it all seems just as impossible as this Adcock business.'

'I'm sorry, I don't see what you're driving at.'

'I said I was thinking in an abstract way. But let me give you a clear-cut chemical problem. Here are your ingredients. A bag of coal. Half a dozen cylinders of liquid air. A sack full of soil dug up out of your garden and a tank of water. Now make that little lot into a human being.'

'What the hell has that to do with it?'

'That's exactly what people are made out of,' I went on, 'carbon from coal, oxygen and nitrogen from the air, water, and a lot of minor ingredients which you can get out of ordinary garden soil. What nature does is to combine these very simple ingredients into a tremendous profusion of living things.'

'There's got to be a lot more to it than that.'

'Only knowing how to do it.'

Harrison was a little more thoughtful now. He sat down and started his usual trick of swinging his legs restlessly.

'Then how is it done?' he asked at length.

'Start with the most primitive idea. Suppose you want to make a tiger. Get hold of an actual tiger and make an exact copy.'

'I still don't see how?'

'You can imagine it. Copying all the pieces—the head, tail, eyes. Rather like a sculptor. Copy every single atom.'

'It would be a hell of a job,' mused Harrison.

'Like copying St Paul's Cathedral stone by stone. Only worse. In fact you wouldn't get very far. But you could imagine it being done.'

'And you think this is what happened with the bees?'

'Something like it.'

'There's got to be more to it.'

'Of course there's more to it. I said this was the simplest idea.'

'Go on.'

'Nature doesn't work this way—it's too hard. Nor does a human builder. When we want to construct something the size of St Paul's we wouldn't dream of doing a literal copy, brick by brick.'

'O.K.,' murmured Harrison, chin dug deep into his chest.

'We work from plans. Plans on sheets of paper. At first sight they bear little immediate relationship to the building. They're abstract. But they carry the information for making the building. Nature works in exactly the same way—from plans.'

'You're not putting it very clearly.'

I took a deep breath and continued, 'Well, every living creature, as well as being a kind of working structure, also carries plans for rebuilding itself. What the biologists call the genetic code.'

'This chromosome business?'

'Yes. An enormous quantity of information is contained in one tiny cell. This gives all the necessary instructions for building your tiger—or a human—or a grain of wheat. When you go from one plant or animal to another the instructions change. But the materials stay the same, more or less so.'

'I understand that. The water and the carbon.'

'It's very interesting when you think about it. When the tiger eats a water-buffalo, the material stays more or less the same. But the instructions change from being water-buffalo instructions to being tiger-instructions. It's simply a case of the same stuff being used in two different ways,' I rambled on.

'Doesn't seem that way to the buffalo,' muttered Harrison.

'No, because each of us only has a single set of instructions. We only have what we are.'

'All right, now what are you getting at regarding Adcock?'

'Can you imagine a creature that has instructions for being more than one thing. Maybe it has instructions to be anything it wants to be. A man, a swarm of bees, anything.'

'I see vaguely what you're getting at. But we don't have creatures of this kind.'

'Not on Earth.'

'Eh?'

'I said not on this planet. We don't have that kind of creature on Earth, which is exactly why the behaviour of R. A. Adcock seems so very peculiar to us.'

'What the hell are you driving at?'

'I'm not driving at anything. I'm asking. I'm asking what would be the ideal way to invade a planet. From the outside. Certainly not with space ships. That's kids' TV material.'

'For God's sake come to the point,' said Harrison, finally throwing himself from his chair in mental agony.

'The ideal way,' I said, slowly collecting my thoughts, 'would be to take up in some way the instructions for building any creature on the planet you were going to. Wouldn't that be the way? You wouldn't have to worry then about whether you'd fit into the normal background of the planet when you got there, whether you'd be able to breathe the atmosphere and a hundred and one other things. You'd know you could do all of them.'

'Because you'd be like the creatures already there,' said Harrison quietly to himself.

38

'Correct. Remember the Martians of H. G. Wells? They came to a sticky end because they were attacked by bugs—terrestrial bacteria. That wouldn't have happened if they'd had the normal built-in resistance of actual terrestrial creatures. And another thing, if anyone were to try and eliminate you, you'd simply change into something else. If Adcock had been put in jail he could have changed into a warder, or even the Prison Governor I suppose—just as he did with the bank teller—Sheppard.'

'West, if what you're saying has the slightest truth behind it, what the hell can we do?'

'I don't know. But I do know that catching those bees, even burning them up with flame-throwers, isn't going to do any good.'

'That's assuming this fairy-tale theory of yours is correct.'

'I wouldn't pin too much on it being wrong. Those bees were too big.'

'What in the name of all that's crazy . . .?'

'They're too big to live long, because of oxygen starvation. But being big certainly gave them a powerful sting,' I said ruefully, examining my still throbbing hand.

'What I want to know is, what are these bees going to change into next, unless they've done it already,' grunted Harrison, opening the office door, as the young radar operator shouted 'Sir, the bees seem to have stopped several miles to the east of Bishop's Stortford, in a place called Hatfield Forest.'

The plot showed exactly this situation.

'Well at least we know they're still bees,' said

Harrison with momentary satisfaction. On sudden impulse I asked,

'What would be the chances of getting to Bishop's Stortford?'

To his credit Harrison made valiant efforts to find out if we could get into the area. From what I could gather in a confused situation, the army had been massively deployed. Troop-carriers and tanks jammed the roads over an area from Ongar in the south to Saffron Walden in the north, from Dunmow in the east to Ware in the west. But against the odds Harrison succeeded in pressuring a military big-wig into securing the necessary free passage for both of us. By now I had the impression he wasn't letting me out of his sight.

But the best laid schemes of mice and men can be brought to naught, as we all know. Another ten minutes and Harrison would have got clean away. Everything was in order, passes and the like, and a car was waiting, when the fellow was called into the office to answer an important telephone call. I knew things had gone wrong the moment he rejoined me in the plotting-room.

'Never argue with the powers that be,' I mimicked.

'Blast 'em. Damn and blast 'em,' was the incisive comment.

Several things had been obvious. First, that Harrison's superiors would eventually catch up with him and would require a top priority report on exactly what all the fuss was about. Second, that although Harrison undoubtedly wanted to keep a tight hold on me he had no authority at the moment to do so. Actually, even before the phone call, I'd already decided to free myself of the man—as soon as I reasonably could. Now I had a heaven-sent opportunity.

'Tough luck, Harrison, real tough luck. But don't worry. I'll report back,' I said, with crocodile tears.

'I'll be damned if you will.'

'You'll be damned if I don't. Give me the car and the passes and I'll report back here some time tomorrow. Otherwise I'm on my way.'

I had the whip hand. I knew it and Harrison knew it. The argument and bluster which followed was a matter of form rather than of substance.

I drove away from Lambolle Road looking first for a newspaper, curiously enough. I was still consumed with astonishment at all this frantic activity. It hardly seemed conceivable that the whole country should suddenly have become appraised of the sinister threat of R. A. Adcock. The newspaper I eventually bought carried a three-inch headline:

MAGISTRATES IN RIOTOUS ASSEMBLY

Photographs occupied more space than words. There was a truly splendid picture of the clerk of the court prancing on the big square table, arms flying, wig thrown high into the air. I have always found it remarkable that whatever the disaster, whatever the place and time, there is always a photographer on hand to record it. The hardihood of the chap who took these particular pictures, in the teeth of the bombing attacks of the swarm of bees, can scarcely be imagined.

The story covered the indecorous court scene at some length but there was no mention of the fate of

Adcock. The key point, the connection between Adcock and the bees, had been missed. I was surprised to find that reporters could be so dumb. But then I could imagine the man-into-bees part of a reporter's story being blue-pencilled by his editor. After long years spent in faking artificial sensation from news that was in no way sensational, editors would be incapable of recognizing the real thing when at last it was thrust under their noses.

How came it that the armed services had been so magnificently deployed? I reasoned as follows. Every commanding officer, be his unit large or small, on land, sea or in the air, is perpetually seeking excuses for action. He wants to get his men doing something instead of forever doing nothing. Routines are invented to keep things moving, but no one is really deceived by a routine. Everybody obeys orders, everybody goes through the motions, knowing it to be one enormous piece of nonsense. But now, after Harrison's dramatic alert, the services were presented with a heaven-sent opportunity really to do something, if only to nobble a swarm of bees.

The affair must have started with the urgent phone call from the Lewisham Civic Hall, a request for a handful of helicopters. But soon the word that a show was 'on' became noised abroad. Other units hungry for action were not to be denied. Within the space of an hour, as squadron followed squadron, as brigade piled on brigade, the operation grew into a vast tidal wave. There they were in their respective plotting rooms, a multitude of moustached faces shouting 'roger' and 'wilco'. I pictured endless rows of armoured vehicles jam-packed throughout the vicinity of Bishop's Stortford.

Laboriously, I crawled my way north along the A11 past Buckhurst Hill. The light was failing rapidly now. The trees parading the edge of the road made up a sinister backcloth. At length, wearisome length, I came on flashing lights which announced the first road-block.

'Evening, sir,' said a policeman as I rolled down my window.

'Not a good evening, officer?'

'No, sir,' said the man sticking his head right in through the window to get a better look at the police radio cramped underneath the dashboard. I took the police pass Harrison had given me and handed it over.

'Rather you than me, sir. Never did like bees,' said the officer switching off his torch and handing the paper back. 'Your best bet would be to go as far as the beginning of the dual carriageway and then turn right. Hatfield Forest is signposted.'

'Are there many more road checks?' I asked.

'That I couldn't tell you.'

The right turn was easily found, a large garage being situated near it, and I made better time along the secondary road which wound a peaceful way through farmland. Hatfield Heath swarmed with military personnel and vehicles. No one seemed particularly interested in my presence there so I drove on slowly across the main A414 and back into the country. Groups of soldiers were sitting by vehicles along the roadside.

I traced and retraced the narrow roads for what

43

seemed an eternity until at last I spotted a signpost into Hatfield Forest. I'd been expecting the name to be written on the white painted arm of a normal signpost. The National Trust pillar had it attached much lower down, which was why I'd missed it before. Another couple of miles brought me to the entrance of the forest. I swung the car onto the verge and got out, glad to stretch my legs after a frustrating drive. It had taken nearly four hours to make only thirty-five miles.

'Halt, who goes there?' came a challenging voice from the dark.

'A friend,' I replied.

'Advance and be recognized.'

I moved across a cattle grid onto what seemed to be an open ride. A powerful light was shone in my face as I approached a group of soldiers.

'What are you doing here?' asked a smoothly tuned voice. I handed over my special military pass. The torch flashed down giving me a chance to adjust again to the dark.

'Dr West?' The torch flashed once more in my face.

'Yes.'

'What can I do for you?'

'I'd like to see the position where the bees were last sighted,' I said, peering through the light in an attempt to see my interrogator.

'That's easier said than done.' The man hesitated while Harrison's note was reread.

'The army can't be responsible . . .' he went on.

'I appreciate that the army can't be responsible.'

'In that case, very good. Thompson, take Dr West to Section 4.'

A young fellow packing a lethal looking weapon came out of the gloom. We walked for some time. The ground was covered with pot-holes, some full of liquid mud. Occasionally I saw the red glow of a cigarette or heard the mumbled curse of a soldier.

'Are you some kind of boffin?' asked the soldier rather shyly.

'Sort of. When were the bees last seen?'

'Around seven, near where we're going. Bloody stupid, calling out the whole bloody army for a swarm of bees. Can't see why they didn't spray the whole place with fly-killer.'

'A reasonable remedy,' I said, wondering whether the powers that be had thought of that one. Something rustled in a bush nearby. Thomson stopped sharply, swung the rifle off his shoulder, and turned his torch on. For a moment we saw nothing. Then in the long grass I noticed a white tail. 'Rabbit,' I remarked. The soldier turned his light off, muttered a short curse and we trudged on.

'Who goes there?' came a whispered command as we turned in amongst some trees and down a narrow path.

'Bloody friend,' answered my guide.

'Advance and be recognized and keep your voice down.'

'Got a guest for you, Sarge,' said Thomson. 'I've got a Dr West. He wants to know where the bees are.'

'All right, Soldier. Dr West, come and join the party.'

Thomson then saluted in the dark and walked away, presumably to rejoin the officer with the well-tuned voice.

'I'm afraid you're not going to see much tonight,' said the Sergeant.

'You saw the bees at about seven o'clock, I believe?'

'Didn't see, just heard. They made a noise like a bloody great engine.'

My eyes were now well adjusted to the gloom. I watched the Sergeant vainly try to illustrate his last statement with a sweep of his arm.

'You've heard nothing since?'

'I should think they're safely tucked up in bed by now,' mused the soldier, 'if they're not dead already.'

'How d'you mean?'

'According to Headquarters they covered the whole of this area with insecticide several hours ago. See.' He pointed his torch at the ground which was littered with dead insects, but no bees.

So they had used insecticide—shutting the stable door, I thought to myself, and said:

'This is going to upset the entomologists.'

'Hm.'

'Have there been any strange noises?' I asked.

'I wouldn't know. The wood is full of noises.'

An hour or so later, when a plane roared overhead, it relieved for a moment the tenseness which the noises of the wood were gradually building up inside me. For a brief while it was man's own world again. Then all I could hear once more was the wind in the trees. Suddenly a long drawn-out howl, rising in pitch, fastened everyone's attention.

'What was that, Sarge?'

'How the bloody hell should I know?'

'Sounded like an animal.'

'Ten out of ten,' grunted the Sergeant caustically.

The howl was repeated, louder this time. Whatever it was couldn't be far away.

'Better take a look.'

'O.K., Sarge, anything you say.'

The men, there were about eight of them, took their weapons from the side of a Land-Rover parked in the open ride. Then we all moved cautiously towards the dense woodland. The creature wasn't far away, nor was it hard to find. The torchlight picked out a white long-haired animal which could best be described as a wolf, although it was on the heavy side for a wolf. Before I could stop him the Sergeant raised his rifle and fired. The creature should have dropped in its tracks, but instead it suddenly seemed as if there were two of them. Sure enough the first animal had been joined by a second. A veritable cascade of small arms fire from the men enveloped the creatures. Like a film effect, the forest was instantly full of them as if the immortal wolves of hell had come to their aid.

I backed off a way as the white wolves came on through the hail of supposedly lethal fire. The soldiers kept up the shooting until the animals were right on top of them. Then again like a film effect the soldiers were gone and the firing stopped. I stumbled desperately out of the woodland, back on to the open ride.

With real luck I found the Land-Rover. Inside it I fumbled for the controls, muttering to myself all the time. The engine burst into life. I had no regard now for anything but to get away. I backed into a tree and then forward, bouncing off young saplings. At the edge of the wood the vehicle was hit by a pack of white bodies. I swung wildly about in an attempt to throw them off. As the machine raced along the pot-holed ride, one of the animals, mounted now on the bonnet, turned its head and looked at me. Then, as if cued, the creature rose on all fours and leapt into the night.

R. A. Adcock had staked out his territory. None among the soldiery would now be willing to dispute him, for guns become useless when they change life, like Circe the sorceress, instead of destroying it. Throughout the hours of darkness the wolves continued to howl, as if in derision at the ways of men.

CHAPTER FIVE

THE SCIENTISTS
EXPRESS AN OPINION

Sunrise was heralded by a deep blue sky. I must have dozed off, slumped in the Land-Rover, for I was awakened by a soldier with a cup of tea and a message enclosed in an official-looking envelope. My eyes felt as though they'd been sand-blasted, so I finished the tea before ripping out an equally official-looking sheet of paper. But it was only from Harrison, demanding that I should return to London forthwith, which in any case had been my intention. With the lightening sky the baying of the animals stopped. The green grass and trees seemed so normal that it was hard now to recall the harassing evil of the night.

Once I was outside the military cordon, the drive back to Lambolle Road took little more than an hour, for it was still early enough to deter even the hardiest of rush-hour dodgers.

'What the devil have you been doing?' asked Harrison as I went in through the back door of the apparently dilapidated building.

'Driving.'

'It's taken the army nearly three hours to deliver a simple message.'

'What's so urgent?' I asked, making a mental note

of the time—seven forty-five according to a clock on the wall.

'You're wanted at a high-level meeting. There's just time to clean up and have breakfast.'

While I was washing and shaving I had an odd notion that R. A. Adcock had dealt with us in a fairly restrained fashion so far. All he'd done in fact was to sting the law and to consume a small fraction of our well-armed, super efficient, super-plus organized army. What really staggered my imagination was the possibility that he, Adcock that is, might elect to become a virulent plague bacillus.

Harrison seemed perpetually busy on the phone, so I made myself a spot of breakfast. From scattered remarks which I overheard it gradually dawned on me that the high-level meeting was to be at Number 10 Downing Street, no less. It was a special convening of the P.M.'s committee of scientific advisers, forced by the morning papers, which at last were carrying the full story.

On the way to Whitehall, Harrison told me he'd faithfully passed on my remarks of the previous afternoon. His superiors in the Security Branch then decided the matter should be reported to the authorities in Whitehall. The intention was to inform a dozen persons at most. But the information wasn't at all of a kind that could be kept secret for long. It wasn't like a secret weapon or a diplomatic pact. It was far too outrageous not to be talked about. Within an hour a score of people knew, then two score. Then the press. So that now it was out and I was on my way to Downing Street, neck ready-shaven for the scientific chopping block.

I'm not by nature a nervous twittering sort of person. But to appear before a committee of the country's top scientists was more calculated to make me nervous than anything else I could think of, especially since they must have read my crazy ideas in cold print.

A battery of reporters and television people were amassed outside Number 10. Harrison applied his shoulder to the human wall and I just followed behind him. He muttered something to the constables at the door, but they insisted he should produce his identification card. Once inside we were shown to an ante-room. A few moments later a young chap, whom I took to be a secretary, came in and said, 'This way, Dr West.'

'From the frying pan into the fire,' I muttered from the doorway. Actually my nervousness was much reduced by the fact that Harrison was not required directly at the meeting. Evidently he had come with me as a guard, which I found irritating.

The interior of Number 10 was considerably larger than I'd anticipated. Acres and acres of wall space were covered with portraits and photographs of past political dignitaries, which gave the place a museum feeling. Perhaps this was the epitaph of the politician: 'We passed through here, never lived, breathed or died here.'

I forced myself back to reality as the door of the Cabinet room was thrust open in front of me. The room itself was much longer than it was wide. I should estimate there were some thirty-five people already there. A few of the scientists I knew by sight. It really was a high flying meeting, for as well as the P.M. there was the Minister of Defence, the Secretary of State for

Science and Education and several junior Ministers. The chair of the meeting was occupied, not by the P.M. himself, but by his chief scientific adviser.

The meeting had clearly been in progress for some time. The difference between being 'called in' to a Committee for a special item and being there from the beginning is always overwhelmingly obvious. Clearly I was the special item.

'We have been acquainting ourselves with Mr Stanton's report,' the Chairman said, looking in my direction.

Who the hell was Stanton? I didn't like to admit I didn't know any Stanton, so I asked if I could see a copy. A glance showed it to contain the substance of all I had told Harrison.

'I'm afraid I don't know Mr Stanton,' I said unguardedly.

'Don't know Stanton! I understand he brought you here this morning!' rapped the P.M., knocking out his pipe noisily.

'I'm sorry,' I said, 'but I know the gentleman as Mr Harrison.'

There were smiles around the table. It was clear from their faces that they thought I was off to a bad start.

'I suggest you speak to the paper,' muttered the P.M.

'Gentlemen, you know as well as I do what the facts are, they speak for themselves in this report of—Mr Stanton,' I began.

'Dr West, I have spent many years reading reports of this, that and the other, which has forced me to the opinion that information about serious matters comes better from the "horse's mouth", so to speak,' said the P.M., showering tobacco over his next-door neighbour.

'Then here are the facts, Prime Minister, as they are known to me. A man walks through a third-floor window and falls fifty feet to the street below. Yet nobody is found in the street. Instead, five minutes later, a swarm of bees the size of golf balls enters the court-room through the broken window. After stinging various members of the court severely, the bees take their leave, making their way north to Hatfield Forest.'

'A long way for a swarm of bees,' interrupted the Minister of Defence.

'It would have been a very long way indeed if the swarm had not secured a lift, on the windscreen of a helicopter named Sunrise. The bees then took to ground in Hatfield Forest, where they were sprayed with insecticide. Because of this the swarm transformed itself to a wolf, or possibly into several wolves. At all events a pack of rampant wolves eventually emerged, as I believe, through the further transformation of military personnel.'

A deathly silence followed, broken at last by the P.M., who said, 'and who will follow that?'

'I'd like to follow, Prime Minister,' responded the Chairman. 'I'd appreciate a little more development of the microbiological side of Dr West's theory. Just how does this creature organize itself biologically?'

'You mean does it change its chromosomes?' I asked.

'Do you know that it does change its chromosomes?' came the sharp reply.

'Personally I think so, but naturally I couldn't be sure.'

'Ah!' said the Chairman, as if an important point had been won.

'What makes you think so, Dr West?' broke in a thin man with flying hair, whom I'd never seen before.

'Allow me a few moments, gentlemen, while I try to develop my ideas on this particular point.'

'Perhaps you'd better,' agreed the Chairman.

I noticed the Professor of Microbiology at the University of Wolverhampton hammering out his pipe in a fair imitation of the P.M.

'I had the idea of a higher stage of sophistication in the organization of life, one that didn't require a chromosomic structure.' This seemed to fall on stony ground, but I continued, 'In much the same way as a programme can exist in a computer at several stages of sophistication.'

An Under-Secretary from the Ministry of Technology gave a long drawn-out 'ah-ah!', for of course computers were Mintech's bailiwick. I waited for the fellow to speak, especially after all his movements and gesticulations, but nothing came forth, so I struggled on.

'You can establish a programme in a fixed structural form on magnetic tape. This is like life in a chromosomic state. In both cases the information is stored in terms of a particular arrangement of material, genes on the chromosomes, magnetic domains on the tape.'

'Professor Hindmarsh is an expert on computers,' spoke up the Mintech Under-Secretary at last.

'Professor Hindmarsh will know programmes can also exist in a high-speed dynamic form,' I said, staring hard at the Under-Secretary, who then took refuge in the doodles before him. 'The information is represented by electrical signals that travel around the computer more or less at the speed of light. It would seem to me that the creature we're dealing with can somehow manage to control the information relating to life in this sort of way.'

'I'm afraid none of us follows the reasoning by which you arrive at this remarkable conclusion,' said the Chairman casually, as though he was hardly listening to my discourse.

'The remarkable effect,' I ploughed on, 'would result partly from the ability of the creature to switch from one life form to another. Switching from one set of chromosomes to another would only be like writing different records on a magnetic tape. And partly from the enormous speed with which the switches take place.'

'Speed?' asked the P.M.

'Yes, speed. It struck me as very strange, even at the time, that several people in the street outside the court saw the man Adcock fall from the broken window yet nobody actually saw the body strike the ground. The next thing to be seen was the swarm of bees.'

'You're not suggesting he changed into the bees while in mid-air?' asked the Minister for Science.

'No, because then the man Adcock would have disappeared in mid-air. Instead he was seen to fall to the ground in the normal way.'

55

'Please go on,' said the P.M. when he saw the Chairman was about to interrupt.

'But if the switch to the bees occurred at the precise moment of striking the ground—if it happened in a flash, possibly less than a hundredth of a second, then nobody could see it. Nobody could see it because it would be too fast for our ordinary human reaction time.'

Just for a fleeting moment I had the meeting with me. Then the man with the flying hair broke the spell. 'If I were running a detective agency, Mr Chairman, I would consider employing Dr West, but I wouldn't consider offering him a post in my laboratory.'

This was the kind of remark peers do not use among themselves but which can be used to squelch an inferior. It was on the tip of my tongue to point out that I hadn't applied for a job in the fellow's wretched laboratory, but my extra-university activities had long ago taught me to hold my tongue—figuratively.

The embarrassed silence which followed was broken after some seconds by a Professor of Astronomy from Cambridge.

'Dr West, how would this invader from outer space get here?'

'Along the light cone,' I replied.

'You mean electromagnetically?'

'I mean along the light cone. All fields, electromagnetic or not, are propagated along null lines—at any rate in vacuo,' I said, determining that I wouldn't give any more simple explanations. The physicists there wouldn't be that worried by these remarks, but the rest would. 'The essential point is that Huyghen's Principle should be satisfied strictly, in order that there be no distortion of information,' I added to make things a little more opaque.

There was a commotion outside a door at the far end of the room, which proved to be only a trolley with coffee. Having negotiated the door two attendants discharged the cups with immense speed and efficiency. I hadn't time to drink more than a mouthful before the astronomer from Cambridge was back to resume the attack.

'Have you any theory as to why the invasion is happening now? Why not last year, or a hundred years ago, or even a million?'

'Because nobody was transmitting radio waves a hundred years ago,' I replied.

There was another longish silence.

'You mean,' said the P.M., 'our own man-made radio transmissions have produced this invasion of yours?'

'Yes, indeed.'

The P.M. puffed away hard at his pipe. Others in the room who had become addicted to this form of smoking made the whole room reminiscent of a flotilla on exercise.

'Sounds to me like a case of environmental pollution,' came a floating statement from the far end of the long table.

'It does look that way,' I agreed, gazing up at the smoke.

'Professor MacCullagh, what are your views?' asked the Chairman, looking down the table in the direction of the former remark. I braced myself, for

MacCullagh was the man I'd been fearing all along. I knew him to be a really top flight physicist.

'Well, I'd like to begin by congratulating Dr West on his knowledge of Huyghen's Principle.' He was smiling, and everyone around the table joined him in some obscure joke. 'The point was actually quite a subtle one, for which I was grateful. Dr West unfortunately is a bit like these extrasensory people. He pins an exceedingly improbable conclusion onto very few facts. There may of course be nothing wrong with this, if the facts are really facts. This to me is the big question of doubt.'

'What have you to say to that, Dr West?' asked the Chairman.

'Only that a whole courtroom saw a man walk through a window . . .'

'Excuse me,' went on MacCullagh, 'a whole courtroom did not see a man walk through a window. You say you did. Mr Stanton may say he did. But the chance that both your memories are faulty is higher—very much higher I would say—than the chance of there being an invasion from outer space. With all respect, Dr West, people make mistakes of this kind every day.'

'But there must be fifty people who will swear a man went through that window.'

'A man went through the window. Let me admit as much. But let me say he went through an open window. Let me say he fell into a blanket of the kind used by firemen, a blanket held by his friends. Let me also say that by the time the people in the street had come to their senses our man had made off with his accomplices in a car. The explanation is prosaic, I'll admit, but 'most reasonable folk would prefer it to yours, Dr West.'

'And a swarm of bees came in through the open window.'

'Yes. Improbable I'll admit. Through the same open window very improbable, but still far more likely than your own explanation.'

'The man went through glass, not through an open window,' I retorted, but without any hope of an understanding with MacCullagh.

'I say the window was open. Possibly the man broke it as he vaulted through. That would not be at all improbable.'

Towards the end of this interchange a message was delivered to the P.M. Through the corner of my eye I saw an expression of pleased satisfaction cross his face.

'But how could people in the street not see several men holding out a blanket?' I asked.

'They wouldn't,' broke in the Chairman decisively. 'Whenever anything unusual happens people always claim to have seen whatever went on. But we definitely know they never really do.'

This style of argument was beginning to get on my nerves. Clever people gone wrong, I thought to myself. A man who I'd taken to be a secretary then spoke up:

'We have indications, sir, that this fellow Adcock was probably in the drug racket. Criminals have escaped before in exactly the way Professor MacCullagh has described. I can't see why we shouldn't work on this basis instead of going way out in the direction of Dr West.'

'Hatfield Forest,' I said. 'You've forgotten the wolves in the forest?'

'My dear Dr West, I am not forgetting the wolves in the forest,' boomed the P.M. 'Gentlemen, I am in a position to give the lie completely to the wolves in the forest.'

Here he waved the paper recently brought to him, in a style uncomfortably reminiscent of Mr Chamberlain.

'I have just learnt that a whole kennelful of Pyrenean mountain dogs escaped last night in the environment of Bishop's Stortford. The dogs escaped into Hatfield Forest it seems!'

My heart sank, for I'd come across this breed of dog long ago. In my undergraduate days I'd roomed with a chap who, unbeknown to the authorities, had one of these creatures. It ate up, quite happily, most of his student grant, and to prevent an untimely death I did my best to feed the poor man, so that in a sense the dog came close to eating up both our grants. Last night if someone had told me that the animals that attacked the soldiers were Pyrenean mountain dogs I would have taken the idea seriously. By nature they're guard dogs, capable of being fierce if attacked. Yet in my experience they are also gun shy, which didn't fit the bill.

'The soldiers fired on them,' I said, looking round the table at the sea of faces.

'I say it with respect, you understand, Dr West,' said the Minister of Defence, 'but soldiers have been known to miss their targets, especially in the dark.'

'Soldiers themselves were lost.'

'Troops are always missing after manoeuvres. They turn up hours, days, or even weeks later.'

At this point the door opened and in came an

attendant leading a vast white Pyrenean. The P.M. consulted his sheet of paper.

'This is Ben,' he said triumphantly. 'He apparently holds the position of kennel leader.'

I smiled, as a thought from the distant past rushed into my mind. It was one of those damp dark days you get in the Midlands. It was the last class of the day. Our teacher was endeavouring to inculcate us with a proper desire to succeed in life, a difficult task as the ink pellets fly. Frenetically she pointed out that every boy who used his time fully and profitably had a chance of becoming Prime Minister of England. 'Joe,' a voice whispered behind me, 'I'll sell you my chance for a bob.'

The dog, let off its lead, walked slowly around the table sniffing each one of us in turn. I was nearly the last. When he reached me the big chap quite deliberately lifted a large paw and gave me a shove in the thigh. I rubbed the dog's throat. Its brown eyes watched me, while it panted, apparently happy with the massage it was getting. Every time I stopped, the paw would shoot out and I'd be forced to carry on.

The human aspect of the gesture made it comic. The tensions of the past hour exploded into loud laughter. The whole table was in an uproar, accompanied now by a veritable cannonade of barking from the dog. Suddenly to me the frivolous atmosphere was gone, for the same sense of the uncanny hit me, as it had done in court at the moment Adcock was brought into dock.

I made my exit just as fast as I could. Grabbing my coat I erupted through the door of Number 10 like a

61

missile hurled from a fifteen-inch gun. My momentum took me flying through the line of reporters and assembled television crews. In fact my violent forward drive carried me the short distance along Downing Street out into Whitehall. Everybody seemed to think I was as nutty as a March Hare, and for my part I felt as if I had walked into *Alice in Wonderland*. Adcock would certainly qualify for the part of the Cheshire Cat.

My story was consistent, but madness is always said to contain its own inner consistency. A madman bends the facts to suit his theory so that in his own mind everything is exactly in place, just like a genuinely valid theory. The difference is that in a valid theory the facts have objective reality.

Whitehall was full of lunchtime walkers. I joined the rush, moving quickly in the direction of Trafalgar Square. Marching slowly along the pavement towards me came a man carrying a placard which read: TODAY IS THE END OF THE WORLD.

'Why is the end of the world today?' I asked as the fellow came alongside me.

'Cause the world is full of sinners and the Lord is coming to rid this world of those who sin against him. Are you a sinner?'

'In the eyes of God I should think so.'

'Then repent and ask his forgiveness.'

'But if the Lord is going to rid the world of people like me how can I be saved by repenting?'

'The God Almighty shows great mercy.'

'You don't think that this new fellow, the Molecule Man, will be in competition with God?'

'That's just politicians' work. They're trying to scare

us into paying more tax, by threatening us with chemical and biological warfare.'

'I entirely agree with you,' I said, turning on my way.

I kept coming back to the committee. Obviously the question was whether I had bent the facts or not. On the face of it the answer ought to be affirmative, because the facts on their face value were ridiculous. But at least there was this to be said for my point of view. Authority had been seriously disturbed, to the extent of convening a high level meeting of scientists in the Cabinet room, and to the extent of a military convergence on Hatfield Forest. I wasn't bending those facts.

Walking across the pigeon-strewn ground between the two fountains in Trafalgar Square I turned casually and saw a heavy man coming towards me at a quickish pace. At first nothing seemed familiar, but then as he came alongside I had the impression of a half-remembered face from somewhere in the recent past.

CHAPTER SIX

PARTY IN THE ELEPHANT HOUSE

The chap managed to puff out, 'Why so fast? They'll have an interesting picture of you on TV tonight, Dr West. None of the usual languid waves of the hand. Face as black as thunder. No sweet smile for the masses, not like Cabinet Ministers and Trade Union bods.'

'You're the fellow who called me a "silly bugger", yesterday in the courtroom,' I said, placing the face.

'Could have been. Jim Taylor of the *Guardian*.'

I shook the extended hand. 'So you're working on the Adcock story?'

'After a fashion. Courtroom dramas are things of my youth. I got myself assigned to the story, because I wanted to find out who is organizing the joke. Somebody must have a sense of humour.'

'Is there any place I can get a sandwich?' I asked.

'There's a pub, just around the corner, about two minutes away.'

I kept silent throughout the short walk as I didn't want to prejudice Taylor's answer to a key question. I kept walking as fast as I could. This was enough to keep my companion quiet. I could hear him sucking in air like a badly adjusted carburettor.

'Afternoon, Tom. Room upstairs free?' he asked of the publican.

' 'Twas last time I looked, Mr Taylor. Your usual?'

'Thank you. Dr West, what would you like to drink?'

'Better make it a pint, I've worked up quite a thirst.'

'I'll be up with it in a moment,' said my host, as we climbed narrow stairs to a small unoccupied room overlooking a small square.

'Mr Taylor . . .' I started.

'Jim.'

'O.K., Jim. You were in court yesterday. How'd you describe the manner in which this R. A. Adcock made his exit?'

'Went straight through the bloody window.'

'Open?'

'No. Jumped up on to the Magistrates' table and from there one step to the window and straight through the glass.'

'You heard the noise of breaking glass?'

'Of course it made a noise. What would you expect when something solid goes through a pane of glass?'

The door opened and our drinks came in. Jim Taylor's down-to-earth Manchester voice removed all possibility that I might have been deceiving myself, unless of course I was imagining Taylor, and the publican, and the pint in my hand. I pinched myself, but then I might have been dreaming the pinch as well.

'What the hell does all this mean?' asked Taylor, sipping his usual, which was some sort of fizzy drink in a large glass.

'There's nothing much I can add to what I read in the morning paper,' I said, raising my glass and taking the first refreshing mouthful of liquid.

'Like hell there's nothing you can add.'

65

'Someone must have leaked a private conversation. It was very frank and confidential so far as I was concerned. Who let it out?'

'Our business,' replied Taylor.

'They should have slapped a "D" notice on it.'

'Should have, but didn't. Security never works when the horse is actually leaving the stable, only after he's already quit.'

'You wrote the piece in the *Guardian*?'

'Sort of.'

'Your headline?'

'Yes,' replied Taylor, putting down his glass with a thump as though preparing to defend himself.

'MOLECULE MEN FROM OUTER SPACE, if I recall it correctly.' Taylor watched me not knowing quite what I was getting at. 'Congratulations,' I said, holding out my hand.

'What for?' he asked, shaking my outstretched hand in some surprise.

'The headline.'

Taylor looked pleased, bashful almost, for there's nothing which puts a reporter more out of countenance than a word of praise. Actually, he deserved it. The name Molecule Man was destined to make history.

'What did they want with that big white dog? They took it in just before you came out looking like a scalded cat.'

'That was a Pyrenean mountain dog called Ben.'

'I don't give a bugger what its name is. What I want to know is what was it doing there?'

'Came from Hatfield Forest, apparently.'

Taylor's eyes focused on mine.

'I see,' he mused.

'What do you see?'

'We start with Adcock, then on through bees and wolves, and now to a dog.'

'In the Cabinet room,' I said unintentionally. Luckily Taylor didn't fasten on to the remark. 'It comes down to watching that dog,' I added hastily.

'Watching the dog,' Taylor muttered, apparently miles away. Suddenly he jumped from his seat, exiting at speed.

I sipped my beer slowly. After an indefinite passage of time it ran out. I thought about another one, but decided I wouldn't for the moment. I tried to arrive at a measure of the depth of intellect of R. A. Adcock. If there was anything in my point of view I simply had to suppose that he worked on a subtler plane than the human mind. This meant it was useless to judge his actions in terms of my own standards. But I could judge him in terms of objective results.

When one looked at results, R. A. Adcock had reached the nerve centre of the country in less than twenty-four hours. He'd done it by changing himself sequentially into a bee, a wolf and a dog. A human does the same thing sequentially by serving years on minor constituency committees; becoming a Parliamentary candidate, often after an internecine party struggle; becoming an M.P. after an electoral battle; becoming a junior minister after several years spent in agreeing with his superiors. At the end of this wholly tedious process, a junior minister might occasionally attend a meeting in the Cabinet room, but even then he wouldn't dare raise his voice to match R. A. Adcock. I remembered the enormous derisive baying bark of the dog as I had taken my hasty leave of the meeting. Rarely indeed has any Minister, however highly placed, given tongue to such a volume of sound. It is true that a human, after his exhausting years of struggle, would naturally have arrived in the Cabinet room in human shape, whereas Adcock had arrived in the form of a dog. But did this matter a hoot if you were an invader from outer space? Being a dog might even seem an advantage. It would at least avoid the need to shave and dress in the mornings.

'Prime Minister's Chief Scientific Adviser has left Downing Street with the dog,' announced Taylor bursting back into the room. This news surprised me more than somewhat. It didn't fit the previous behaviour pattern of R. A. Adcock. After achieving the ultimate, by arriving so triumphantly at the nerve-centre of affairs, why had he permitted himself to be led away by the Prime Minister's Chief Scientific Adviser? To my human intellect there was inconsistency here. But there was also inconsistency in judging Adcock on a merely human level. This was a pitfall I told myself that I must try and avoid. It was to be expected that an excellent reason for being led away by the Prime Minister's Chief Scientific Adviser would eventually emerge.

'You'd better put a tail on this fellow and on the dog,' I remarked somewhat distantly.

'I've done that already,' said Taylor, handing over another pint of beer. 'I've got his schedule for the afternoon too. The annual Zoo party.' He then downed most of a second fizzy drink in a fair imitation of the Falls of Niagara.

'He's giving the party, the Chief Adviser?' I asked incredulously.

'Correct.'

'Can you get me a press ticket? I don't think I'm persona grata just at the moment.'

Taylor thought for a moment, then finally drained his glass. 'Come on, we haven't all day,' he rumbled, stifling a belch and waving a finger at my half-finished beer. 'Press pass,' he kept muttering as we descended the rickety wooden stairs.

'Look, if it's going to be this much of a bother . . .'

'My dear Dr West, no trouble at all, no trouble.'

From the pub to his office was only a few hundred yards. He left me in the lobby entrance and took a small old-fashioned elevator upstairs. So it had come round to the Zoo's annual party again. I knew, second hand, that the party is considered an outstanding social event. London's élite would be invited. Maybe I was becoming genuinely harebrained, but this animal business was beginning to get me down. Suppose Adcock produced a ruckus at the Zoo, culminating in the consumption or transformation of London's élite? It seemed that my light-hearted conversation with Stanton-alias-Harrison about the water buffalo might be coming home to roost with a vengeance.

Taylor came racing down a flight of stairs disdaining the lift, looking for all the world like a boy with half a day off. 'Here you are, straight from the forgers' press,' he said thrusting a press card into my hand. 'Thanks,' I said, placing it in my top jacket pocket.

Taylor, considering his weight problem, was remarkably fast over the ground. We both searched the two-way traffic for a vacant cab, but were out of luck.

'That will do us.' Taylor grabbed my arm and pointed to a double-decker bus as it came lumbering along. 'Fine,' I agreed, looking around for a stop sign. But Taylor had other ideas. First he pushed me off the pavement far out into the street. The front of the bus passed too close for comfort. Then as the rear entrance came abreast, he stuck out an arm and grabbed the centre pillar. I was only a fraction of a second behind him. My arm straightened and I was yanked violently off my feet. Luckily Taylor gave me a firm tug, so that I ended in the bus instead of sprawling in the road.

'You don't travel often by bus,' he muttered as we mounted to the upper deck. 'Not your way,' I said, groping unsteadily for a seat beside him. 'Only way to get around.' Here Taylor pointed to the queue which stood patiently at the next stop.

'All right, there's one behind,' called the conductor as he let two young women on.

'See what I mean, we'd have been there for hours.'

I lapsed into silence, nursing my aching arm, until the bus reached Euston Road. Taylor then got up and simply threw himself off as we passed one of the southern entrances to Regents Park. I followed him as best I could, somehow keeping my balance as my feet hit the road.

A short walk now took us into the Park. As we neared the Zoo we were treated to a curious vignette. A television outside-broadcast van was parked near the Zoo entrance. Some yards away, a sheep-skin coated reporter was interviewing passers-by. We stopped and listened.

'Madam, what d'you think about the Molecule Man?' asked the reporter, flashing his microphone close to the nose of a large passing woman. She swept past him as undeviating as a battleship.

'You, sir, you've heard about the Molecule Man?'

'Political, if you arsk me.'

'How do you mean?'

'Course it's political. Everything's political these days.'

'And you, Madam, what does this Molecule Man story mean to you?' cried the frustrated reporter, scurrying across a path to catch a young woman dragging her two young children.

'Bloody papers!' she exclaimed. 'Why didn't they make sure they'd got toys in the shops before letting go with that story. Ever since my husband told the kids this morning I've had nothing but trouble. Can't find any Molecule Men in the shops.'

Then along came a jaunty fellow in a flat-topped cloth hat and a vivid yellow sports jacket.

'Sir! What do you think of the Molecule Man?' The man straightened himself up, dragging at the same time his bashful girlfriend into the full view of the camera, 'All I got to say is, I bin made of molecules all mi' life, 'aven't I. Good luck to 'em I say.'

'Why d'you say good luck to 'em?'

'Brightens things up. Never a dull moment. Makes a bloody good change from the mess things are in, don't it?' Then he was gone, a huge grin on his face.

'Come on, we still have to get you into this place,'

said Taylor. He bought two entrance tickets. Inside, animals grunted and groaned as we walked round. At first I had the impression that Taylor was taking me on a conducted tour of the Zoological Gardens but at length we came to an office. 'Here, better give me your press card,' he said, reaching into my top pocket, 'you might be recognized.'

Animals in the cages around the office looked forlornly at me as I stood first on one leg and then on the other.

'They've got a bloody parrot in there,' said Taylor as he reappeared, 'and the only phrase it knows is "wait your turn". Here take these. We might get separated.' He handed me both the press card and an invitation to the party.

'I suppose it'll be crowded.'

'All these bun fights are so crowded it's like the Albert Hall on the last night of the Proms, coupled with a weekend night at The Prospect of Whitby.'

'Where now?'

'The Elephant House.'

'A party in an Elephant House!'

'Last year it was the Aviary, this year it's the Elephant House. Can't be too careful when you deal with politics, especially animal politics.'

'How about the P.M.'s Chief Scientific Adviser?'

'He's here,' said Taylor.

'With the dog?'

'With the dog. Follows him everywhere apparently.'

Reaching the Elephant House, we shouldered our way through a crowd of people blocking the entrance.

They fell back as Taylor shouted 'Press, Press!' It wasn't the elephants, it was elegantly dressed people, tripping around the concrete floor of the House, that was providing the attraction.

'Quite a sight,' my companion remarked as we both paused a moment to take in the view. 'The Zoo would make a fortune if this went on all the time.'

A policeman checked our invitations and press cards. He had a faint smile and an expression which could have been read as meaning 'poor stupid sods'.

'Excuse me a second,' yelled Taylor, spying some friends.

'Not at all,' I shouted above the din, watching a white-coated waiter with a tray of drinks progressing measuredly through the crush. 'If you need some help, shout,' roared Taylor, vanishing into the thick of the mob.

Elegant dresses, hats, whiffs of perfume floated through my consciousness. From time to time I caught glimpses of my waiter. At last I communicated to him that a glass of whatever he had on the tray wouldn't come amiss. The fellow saw my plight and with an informing nod of his head virtually guaranteed that next time round I might get one. A woman standing amongst a crowd of jabbering people seemed to get a different idea of what my sign language meant. I watched her and she watched me. Then with little ceremony she pointed at herself and at me. I nodded, but she decided to play hard to get and turned back to her group.

Stanton-alias-Harrison pushed his way through the dense pack of bodies. 'Rough time, I hear you had this morning,' he said, waving an empty glass.

'I did indeed, Mr Stanton.'

'Oh, since I started as Harrison let's keep it that way.'

'Fine, are you celebrating?' I pointed to the empty glass.

'In a way. You'll be pleased to hear the case is now closed. The files on it will be guarded only by cobwebs and the dust of time!'

'Hang on, I'll get you another drink,' I said, spotting my waiter struggling through the bodies with his tray.

'Sorry, sir, it's like surviving in a tank of sharks. What I don't know is what they do with the glasses,' he said, offering me a tray with only three on it.

'Not to worry.' I took them all. 'If you could manage another trip I'd be grateful.'

The fellow smiled wearily and started battling his way back to depot. I held the glasses high, moving as near as I could to the woman I'd had the sign talk with. I started it again, once I had her attention, by nodding at the drinks in my hand. She smiled approvingly and stuck up five fingers.

'Good man,' said Harrison, relieving me of a glass.

'We should have some more in a moment.'

'Have you come to see whether Ben behaves himself?'

'Ben?' I said, looking in the direction of the elephants.

'Ben, the dog. The dog that seems to have the government in tow.'

It struck me that Harrison had somehow got rid of his original glass. I waited until he finished the second drink and then offered him my third. With interest I saw him turn and carefully lob the empty glass into a pile of thick straw.

'Very simple when you know how.'

'You still don't believe this dog Ben is as innocent as they think?' I asked.

'Adcock's got everybody in his pocket. Everything we do to discredit him seems to turn out in his favour. Bloody scheming criminal, even if it does seem unlikely that he came from outer space,' he concluded.

I spotted my waiter again and made after him, but to no purpose this time. Frustrated, I looked around for the dog. At length I saw him surrounded by a coterie of admirers. I strolled around as best I could and came eventually to a vantage point from where I could at last see the elephants. Of course they had their own quarters separating them from the guests. An interesting notion occurred to me. Why did we consider the elephants to be in a cage whereas this milling throng of humans considered themselves to be free? On the face of it, looking around me, there was nothing to define which was the cage and which was freedom. There was just a single fence dividing the House into two parts, one for the elephants, the other for humans. Of course it was the world outside the Elephant House that defined the cage. It was because there was an outside, an outside world in which we humans moved, but the elephants didn't, that made us think of the elephants as caged.

If I was right in my view of R. A. Adcock, then he had a world outside the earth, whereas we humans did not. So to Adcock it would seem, ironically enough, that we humans were the ones in the cage. Maybe he saw little or no difference between us and the elephants.

I glanced back in the direction of Ben. He was being patted on the nose by an elderly woman. A man standing alongside the woman attempted to get Ben to shake hands with his paw. Not succeeding, he took hold of Ben's paw and shook it. To Ben it seemed as if a game had started. He was suddenly down on his chest, his lips drawn back to snarl, rump stuck high in the air with the furthest extremity of the tail waving around.

It was then that one of the elephants let out a great trumpeting. Ben turned in its direction, ears cocked, tail high. In a flash he was racing up and down the fence, challenging the elephants.

'For God's sake do something,' came a frightened voice behind me, for obviously the elephants were becoming uneasy at the snarling dog. Inevitably, there came a still louder trumpeting, which seemed to Ben a final challenge. The latticework of the fence gave the dog's paws a fair amount of purchase. A jump took him about six feet. The enormous strength of the animal kept him going, up and up, until incredibly he reached the top, a good ten feet above the ground. In a flash he was down among the elephants, snarling and raging.

But Ben was no match for the big forwards of the animal world. They adopted exactly the crowding tactic used for dealing with tigers or leopards. They formed up in line abreast and advanced slowly on the dog with the clear intention of crushing him. At this point three keepers rushed in through a door behind the elephants. When their entrance brought a cheer from the crowd, I had the absurd feeling that I was part of a slap-stick comedy from the days of silent films.

'What the devil's going on?' said Harrison at my elbow. 'Looks like backstage before the Royal Variety Performance,' remarked Taylor, joining me at the same moment.

'Watch the show if you like, but I'm getting out,' I said, starting to move away. Too late. The menacing line of elephants reached the dog. One moment there was a flash of white, then no white. At this point there came a deafening roar from the elephants. I looked hard but the dog had vanished in a matter of seconds and a solid phalanx of elephants was battering away at the lattice fence. It was designed so as not to be pushed down by several leaning animals, not to withstand the sort of onslaught it was receiving now. Almost like paper the fence tore from its fastenings.

Astonishingly then, the elephants paused, parted ranks to reveal an enormous white bull.

'Bloody hell,' shouted Taylor in my ear. The party turned immediately into a free for all. No question of women and children first. There was a wild shrieking stampede for the exits, devil take the hindmost. The big white elephant cocked his ears and moved forward. Although the mad human scramble for the exit became still more frenzied, I had the curious impression that the elephants weren't really interested in the people but in getting out themselves. The bull elephant, with more trumpeting, and with a swing of his trunk indicating the bars of the House, set them to work. Like an experienced demolition crew they stood in line, trunks round the bars, and heaved in rhythm together. With a loud and ominous crack the whole front of the House gave way.

'Bloody marvellous,' grunted Taylor, picking himself out of some debris, 'come to a party expecting to ruin your suit with booze and end up covered with cement dust.'

The animals had gone, rampaging into the outside world. It was we humans, at least those of us who had not managed to get through the exit, who were now left in the cage. We made a fine sight, sobbing, frightened men and women in total disarray. It was the speed of events that shattered us. One moment we were chattering among ourselves in our usual polite, civilized, naïve way. Seconds later and the normal world had wholly collapsed. It must be the same in a big earthquake. The scale of violence goes outside normal tolerance.

Probably because we were expecting trouble, Taylor, Harrison and I recovered more quickly than the others. Taylor, looking ten years older from the grey dust in his hair, shot off to find a phone, followed closely by Harrison and myself. We weren't too far from the route taken by the elephants, so it was easy for us to reach the outside world. It was clear there had been plenty of trouble. The elephants, bunched together, had cut a veritable swath through the Zoo. A cacophony of car horns floated across Regents Park. I concluded that the elephants had projected themselves into the early evening traffic, and I marvelled at R. A. Adcock's remarkable sense of timing and showmanship.

CHAPTER SEVEN

R. A. ADCOCK HOTS UP THE PACE

Harrison and Taylor left me on urgent business, Taylor obviously to write his copy. I had a feeling I'd had about enough of R. A. Adcock. Probably because of lack of sleep the previous night I was becoming querulous. I walked out through the smashed entrance turnstiles, following almost automatically the path of destruction. Reaching the outer road round the park, I headed south. The elephants had certainly judged their exit extremely well, for the evening traffic was starting to thicken. Everyone knows how just one traffic light can be enough to snarl up traffic to an almost unbelievable degree. Even without anything untoward happening a single roundabout can make its influence felt a couple of miles away. London rush-hour traffic operates at the very margin of mobility. Add the slightest overload and it stops altogether. So you can imagine the effect of projecting a herd of frenzied elephants into it.

The traffic itself had the natural effect of gradually dividing up the herd from one unit into many individuals, so that instead of a single blockage soon there were many. Finchley Road apparently was the first to seize, with consequences that spread quickly south across Euston Road. With Euston Road hopelessly blocked, within a short time all traffic north of the river was at a standstill.

Drivers in their cars on Euston Road, realizing they were stuck for some time, were turning their engines off.

'I say there, have you any idea of what's holding us up?' a well-dressed gent asked me as I walked past. I stuck my head through the open window of his car to answer him.

'I understand the authorities intend to keep it a secret for as long as possible, but at the risk of breaking the Official Secrets Act I'll tell you. It's elephants.'

The man gave me a furious scowl, turned to a fellow passenger saying, 'He's mad,' just at the moment a bellowing elephant came charging along the pavement on the opposite side of the road.

'Yes, elephants,' I nodded to the stunned gent and crossed the road, following in the wake of the animal.

Normally, I supposed, Zoo keepers would have dealt with the crisis by driving around with tranquillizer rifles. Now, owing to traffic blocking the streets, they would have to keep to their feet. This would be quite useless because the elephants could force their way through the chaos at a considerably faster pace than the keepers. It seemed equally hopeless to hunt the creatures from the air. As far as I could see the elephants now had London at their mercy.

I thought of making my way to Liverpool Street, and of returning to Cambridge. I tried to get into the tube station at Oxford Circus but the queues were so enormous that I soon lost heart. Despondently, I walked on towards Marble Arch. I noticed a café and went in just to wait out the traffic congestion. Because others had the same idea it took quite a time before I acquired a coffee, which had to be drunk with great care, standing in a jostling throng. Through the café window I saw a bike racing past piled high with papers. At least the newspaper people seemed to have a few useful ideas. Since delivery vans couldn't be used, they'd obviously hired every boy with a bicycle to do the job for them. A news vendor on the far side of the street also had ideas. He was holding up a board so that we could all read the headline:

MOLECULE MEN DISGUISED AS ELEPHANTS
SABOTAGE LONDON TRAFFIC.

'What film are these Molecule Men in?' a young woman in the crowd asked her friend. 'They're getting a hell of a lot of publicity.'

'Don't know,' was the reply, 'but it should be good when it comes out.'

Every traffic jam finally sorts itself out. It isn't hard to understand how the knot eventually becomes untied. First the existence of the jam becomes widely known. Then with the spreading news the chaos is left to itself. Nobody tries to come into it from outside. At the same time there is an efflux from the perimeter, slow at first but gathering momentum. So at length the pressure eases at the centre and the jam at last loosens itself.

This is exactly what happened now to the motor traffic. But as the motor traffic managed to get clear of Central London a new phenomenon set in. The vehicles were replaced by people, especially by students. Thousands upon thousands of people appeared in the streets from the Underground system. I watched from the pavement outside the café.

'Where are you going?' I asked one long-haired individual as he floated past.

'Trafalgar Square, Man, get into the groove and beat it down there,' came the languid reply.

I battled my way through the crowd back to Oxford Circus. Banners could be seen demanding a fair deal for students. From the direction of Tottenham Court Road I heard a cheer, repeated and repeated again. Then along the middle of the street came a procession. Prancing in front of the procession was the big bull elephant. The creature snatched up one of the student banners and thrust it high in the air, the proclamation reading:

WE DEMAND PARTICIPATION

Somewhere behind, a brass band started to play 'Land of Hope and Glory', and the procession swept along towards Piccadilly Circus. A fellow blowing away on a tuba passed me. I started after him, 'How come the band?' I shouted as I drew level.

'Was meant to be a brass band concert at Albert Hall,' he said from the corner of his mouth.

'What happened?'

'Most of us got stuck at the station down the road. We just joined in.' He pointed at the crowd.

The band started in real earnest now. Amazedly, I watched the white elephant dancing its way down Regent Street to the sound of the 'Washington Grays'. Reaching Piccadilly Circus, we were joined by crowds

surging in from all directions. More and more bandsmen managed to find each other. The elephant did a
tour of the Circus, as if to make sure that we were all
present and in attendance. Meanwhile a couple of
policemen stood guarding the doors of Barclays Bank.

Suddenly the crowd moved again. Not wishing to be
crushed I went with it, down the Haymarket and on to
Trafalgar Square. My section of the crowd swept
through Cockspur Street wedging itself in and around
Admiralty Arch. I thought the elephant had turned into
the Square via Pall Mall East, but this was only an
impression, since by now I'd lost sight of it. A silence
swept over the vast crowd. In the distance I heard a
voice. I listened but could make out very little of what
was said.

'It's Gwynn Davies talking,' shouted a Welshman
close by.

'I hope he's givin' it to them,' remarked his companion, a small powerfully built scrum-half type.

'What is Mr Davies talking about?' I asked.

'The case for Welsh independence, what else now?'

'How did the elephant get into the act?'

'A fine idea it was, to change from the dragon to the
elephant.'

Somewhere from up front there came another enormous cheer which almost drowned the last remark of
my scrum-half friend. The cheering went on and
on seemingly for several minutes. Then for the
second time the band played the Washington Grays.
The crowd swayed gently backwards and forwards to
the sound. A girl linked arms with mine and started
me moving in time to the music. I felt as though I were

being initiated into the art of marching. Suddenly the crowd around Admiralty Arch parted and the white elephant came through, followed by a multitude of musicians, instruments to their mouths. Once through the gate the elephant reared up onto its hind legs, trunk held high above its head, still holding a banner. I watched with astonishment as I'd only seen elephants performing in this way in circuses. The elephant remained on his two rear feet and literally started doing a majorette's drilling down the middle of the Mall.

'Man, this is wild,' came a comment from close by.

'Come on,' said the girl, our arms still interlinked, 'I want to get up behind that elephant.' So we pushed our way through the moving crowd in front of us. After a certain amount of shoving and bustling we reached the band behind the elephant. The procession turned left and we proceeded past Horse Guards Parade, past various government buildings, then left again into Parliament Square. Police took up positions to stop us invading Parliament. The elephant I suppose could easily have pushed through them and gone a-trumpeting into the Chamber. But it elected to halt in front of the entrance steps. The musicians formed themselves in a deep ring around the creature. The Square was now solid with people. Night had descended long ago. With a curious prescience I wondered why the authorities didn't turn out the lighting, leaving us all in unco-ordinated darkness. At any rate they didn't. Like music in 4/4 time, first beat there was silence, unbroken by traffic noise. Next beat, the elephant bellowed defiance at the police. Then came a blaring fanfare from the musicians, and finally a massed roar from the crowd:

BRING OUT YOUR DEAD

After frequent repetition of this pattern it at last became clear that M.P.s were not accepting our advice, since not one of them appeared.

Then we were away again marching around Parliament Square and out along Birdcage Walk. I noticed as we progressed that our leader, the white elephant, had rid himself of part of the banner, retaining only a wooden pole which he was now using most effectively as a baton. Every so often the sound of the band would die momentarily away when I could hear his hooves beating out a tremendous rat-a-tat-tat on the roadway.

We must have been halfway along the Walk when a sound like thunder came from overhead. Although the street lights gave excellent visibility along the road we were quite blinded to what was happe ing above us. The shock of overwhelming sound stopped the band.

The players made no attempt to restart their music after the noise had died away. In fact during those few moments the elephant accelerated his pace. We all moved forward as fast as we could, but even so he began to go well ahead of us.

I had the impression there were three planes, but really it wasn't possible to count them. At first I thought their intent was merely to buzz us. I kept going forwards as fast as I could, separated now from the girl, and well clear of the bandsmen who were handicapped by their instruments. Suddenly I saw red splotches jumping around on the pavement thirty or forty yards ahead.

'They're firing at us,' I yelled to nobody in particular. 'Bloody maniacs,' I went on, my mind paralysed by this outrageously drastic way of breaking up the parade.

The elephant was still forging strongly ahead, in the direction of Buckingham Palace. To the men in the planes the creature must have been an easy target. The third run came in. I saw tracers and cannon shells start well short of the animal. It seemed an eternity, but it can only have been a second or two before the raking fire reached the elephant. I watched as the big fellow leapt into the air, mortally hit, bellowing in the rage of death. At the same precise instant a brilliant flash came from all sides, followed by total darkness.

CHAPTER EIGHT

THE WHISPERING WIND

For just a few seconds I thought I'd been hit myself, hit and blinded. Then looking upwards I saw starlight. With intense relief, I walked from the roadway to the flanking grassy parkland, where I simply flopped down. Minutes later I began to feel chilly, so I got to my feet, wondering what to do. The lights ought to come on as soon as the circuit was repaired. But nothing seemed to be happening. I moved towards the centre of the park, looking for a bench, and trying to figure out how the failure of the electricity could be connected with R. A. Adcock. Lack of sleep from the previous night was catching up with me now. I found no bench, either because it was too dark or because there weren't any, which I found hard to believe. I still had the aimless idea of going home to Cambridge, even though the last train must have left long ago. I decided to walk to Liverpool Street, making my way in what I considered to be the direction of the Mall. I took several wrong turnings, stumbling over flower-beds and bushes before I extricated myself from the park. The Mall, at least I assumed it was the Mall, was full of quietly walking people. This dark calm made strange contrast with the uproar which had preceded it. These shadows I supposed were simply going home. Distances to even outlying

87

districts like Wimbledon and North Hendon seem a long way, but they were within the walking range of most people. But I could hardly walk fifty miles or more to Cambridge. Only now did I realize that I would have to sit or stand around until morning.

I tried to grasp the scale of what was happening. The great city of London in total darkness, thousands—perhaps hundreds of thousands—of people slowly making their way home, or back to their offices or to friends who lived in Town. I thought of the streets, avenues and roads, crawling with groping, stumbling humanity, quietly cursing, or not so quietly, as the blisters appeared. Yes, R. A. Adcock had made his mark on us all right.

Gradually the streets cleared. In all this time there had been no sight nor sound of police cars, ambulances, fire engines or other public vehicles. This increased my presentiment that an uncanny hand had taken a grip on the life of the city.

I walked more or less at random and somehow ended up in the park again. This time I found a bench and settled down to wait until daylight. My mind wandered over the events of the evening. Time and time again I returned to the apparently insuperable difficulty of connecting Adcock with the blackout. Always I hit the same basic problem—how to grasp the point of view and the motives of a creature from another time and place. To us, the elephant, while respectworthy, is nevertheless an inferior animal. But R. A. Adcock might see little difference between an elephant and a human. Taking the shape of an elephant might not seem any more of a comedown to him than taking the shape of a man.

But undeniably we had one real point of contact. R. A. Adcock plainly had a mordant sense of humour. Walking through windows, stinging bees, wolves, Ben in the Cabinet room, the white tap-dancing bull elephant, and now this dark silence. It was all part of a pattern. Adcock just had to have a part in this blackout but I was completely at a loss to see how or where.

Sleep overcomes us all at times when we least expect it. I was awakened by the birds heralding the new morning. Sunrise wasn't far away. My back ached from the hard, unyielding bench. My neck was stiff. I shifted my now-aching body to a vertical position and tried to stretch the pain away. Seeking to ease the stiffness from my joints I walked towards Birdcage Walk. Suddenly the pain was gone. I gazed towards the end of the Walk in astonishment. There, rearing high into the sky, was a grove of enormous trees. Less than ten minutes of hard walking brought me to them. Only then, in the dark interior of the grove, could I espy the façade of Buckingham Palace.

I stood for a long moment just taking in the fantastic sight. I examined the soft springy, very thick red bark. There was no doubt about it. The trees were sequoias, giant sequoias. I tilted my head back to get a view of the tops, a good three hundred feet up in the air. There was absolutely no doubt about it. A quick count put the number at roughly a hundred, with the Palace sheltering like a doll's house in the centre of the grove. In fact the Palace now had a kind of Central-European Christmas look about it, the wood-cutter's children-in-the-forest sort of thing.

The tops of the trees were whipping in the wind,

89

but so tall were they that only a gentle whispering could be heard at ground level. Dimensionally, I suppose they were eight to twelve feet across the trunk. There was an impelling dignity about them—a dignity in remarkable contrast to the rip-roaring white elephant.

It was almost half an hour before I saw anyone. I spent the time just walking about. There had been a corresponding change in the ground, from the hard asphalt of the road and the cobbles of the Palace forecourt to soft ground with deep humus. It was quite silent underfoot. I kicked an eighteen-inch cone. The effect of the whispering wind in the tree tops, of the soft silent floor of the grove, was eerily odd. It was also odd that nobody was about. Of course at five o'clock of a June morning you don't expect many people about. But this was central London after all. It would be normal to find an occasional passing car or taxi. I supposed the appalling traffic pile-up of the previous evening, the failure of the electricity supply and the fact that most people living in the London area had whooped it up last night, and were now sunk in sleep, explained the situation. Even so, I had the conviction that I was still missing the key part of the puzzle.

The palace guard came marching through the trees. It was like a television programme with the sound turned down, for there was no noise. The men faced each other, twiddled their rifles with mechanical precision, nodded their busbys, and then retreated back from whence they came. The spectacle was most peculiar because of my now distorted sense of scale. We're all used to the fact that our sense of scale changes when we go outdoors. An exceedingly large room seems tiny if you lay its area on the open ground outside. Among very great trees you change your outdoor scale still further. You set everything by the trees. This makes all everyday man-made objects quite insignificant. Now it had the effect of turning the Palace guard into minuscule figures no larger than toy soldiers.

Shattering the silence came the whining of lorry gear boxes and four-wheel drives. Down the Mall rumbled four large army trucks. The things stopped short of the trees and proceeded to disgorge fifty or more soldiers. As I watched I heard more trucks roaring away in the direction of Hyde Park.

'Sir!' a voice shouted, near enough to make me jump.

'You gave me a fright,' I said to a young lieutenant.

'Sorry, sir, but I've got orders to clear and cordon off the area.'

'Why?'

'Those are my orders, sir.'

'But the palace guard is still on duty.'

'Sorry, sir. I wouldn't know anything about that, sir.'

'Remember the battle of Hatfield Forest?' I asked.

'I wouldn't know anything about that either, sir. I just have orders to clear, cordon and contain this area,' continued the soldier in his parrot-like style.

'You do that. Contain them if you can.'

With what I hoped sounded like a threat, I walked off in the direction of Hyde Park. I would have preferred to stay but there was no way through the lieutenant's particular brand of mental undergrowth. Halfway along Constitution Hill I turned and glanced back at the magnificent redwood grove.

Suddenly I discovered that I was extremely hungry.

Not surprising considering the lack of food on the previous day. My thoughts were divided in about equal parts between thinking about the trees and food. No restaurants or cafés would be open for another couple of hours. The best chance would be room service at an hotel. I headed therefore towards Park Lane.

Obviously the idea of the military was to clear a wide area around the redwoods. My guess was that the authorities would be aiming at cutting and carting them away before the morning was over. Otherwise there might be an outcry to keep 'em. To a military commander, removing a hundred trees in six hours would seem a simple enough operation—until he woke up to the size of these enormous fellows. Getting them down would present tricky problems. It was heavy odds that nowhere in the country would there be tackle big enough for a job like this. It might be safe to suppose that it would take a week, even weeks, to remove them. In that length of time anything might happen.

This reasoning pleased me. I pushed my way through the swing door of the Dorchester.

'Would there be any chance of something to eat?' I asked the porter.

'Sorry, sir, the kitchens aren't open yet.'

'Could you have a look?' I persisted, slipping a note into his hand.

'You never know, sir. Just let me take a look,' was the instant response.

'I'll be over there,' I said, pointing to a seat. The main lounge was full of crumpled up figures in various stages of modest undress. I lifted a pair of well-polished shoes carefully from a hard-backed chair and sat down. As I looked around at the bowlers, pin-striped suits and brief cases, I wondered how much the management charged for a place in this temporary bedroom.

'You the gentleman who wanted breakfast?' asked a small woman dressed in a raven's costume, well-suited to a voice as hoarse as a crow.

'I'm extremely hungry, yes,' I replied quietly.

'Been out all night?'

I nodded.

'The whole place seems topsy turvy this morning. Come on, we're going to have all this lot clamouring for breakfast soon.'

Eagerly, I followed through the lounge, across the dining-room, and into the kitchen. It was quiet and clear there, still awaiting the commotion of the day's work.

'Coffee or tea?'

'Coffee,' I replied after some deliberation. 'Are there any spare beds?'

'Silly question. If there were any beds there'd be no people out there. The coffee's in the big tin.'

The tin was of instant coffee. I spooned some powder into a silver jug and added steaming hot water. Meanwhile the Raven had a large frying pan nestling on the range with bacon and egg jumping up and down in the bubbling fat.

'Why are you doing this for me?' I asked, pouring myself a cup of coffee.

'That's my business. If you want a reason though, maybe it's because I like your face,' she said, levering my breakfast out of the pan.

'That doesn't make sense—in my case.'

'When you think about it, nothing makes sense. I'd just settled down to watching a bit of telly last night, when boom, everything goes black. I'll tell you this, those malarkies in that school house down in Westminster won't be getting my mark next time,' she exploded like the fat in the frying-pan.

'What d'you think of these Molecule Men?' I asked, mouth full.

'Well, as far as I can see these fellows enjoy life, have a prank and that sort of thing. But mind you they can't be outside the law. Fair's fair. We'll have to be protected, us people in the street.'

'What would you do with them?'

'Leave 'em alone. They won't bother us if we don't bother them.'

'But they might be from outer space. Perhaps they've come to take over the world.'

'Then thank Gawd, I say. It's about time things was less serious, so we can relax. The war's been over for years and in all that time we've had nothing but problems. It's about time we had a bit of fun.'

The telly really must be doing a promotion job for R. A. Adcock, I thought.

After my breakfast the Raven hurriedly pushed me back into the lounge which was now beginning to stir. One tall thin individual vacated a sofa which allowed me to sit soft for a while. As I was drowsing away the extraordinary significance of the redwoods suddenly hit me. Reluctantly I quit the sofa and went off to explore the men's cloakroom. Here I had a quick wash, shave and brush down from another hotel employee who responded in the same friendly fashion as the hall porter had done. Then outside into the street. A taxi was standing there.

'Ten Downing Street,' I said somewhat self-consciously.

It was of course very likely that the P.M. would refuse to see me, but it was worth a try. After all I had been right in my theory, at any rate in part of it, which gave me some claim to be heard.

'Like to see the trees, Guv? There's a bloody great Jack-an'-the Beanstalk down by the Palace.'

'All right, let's hope we see the giant.'

'That would make my day, that would. Trouble is they've got the back streets closed off.'

'How about Birdcage Walk.'

'That as well, they say they're laying some new road up there.'

I wasn't surprised. Evidence of the cannon shells wouldn't look too good by daylight. We stopped by the Victoria Memorial. The place was swarming with military, just as I'd expected. A private with a lead-spraying rifle on his shoulder soon moved us on.

'Bloody 'ell,' groaned the cabby with a sweeping gesture. 'I pays for that. I pays for 'is gun and 'is uniform. I pays for 'is bloody ox and I pays for his bloody ass. Then what does he do? He bloody well moves me on.'

'I think they're going to cut them down,' I remarked casually.

The taxi shuddered to a halt. The driver turned slowly in his seat and fixed me with an incredulous gaze. 'Say that again, Guv?'

'I said they're going to cut those redwoods down.'

Again there was a groan. The man turned and the cab moved forward.

'Chop 'em down!' he shouted back at me after a moment's pause. 'I'll tell yer this. Those trees are worth millions. To us taximen they're a licence to print money. Going to Downing Street you say. Well you tell his nibs that 'enery 'orsefield here thinks he's gone barmy. You can give him my excretions too.'

Public opinion seemed to have the right idea, I reflected as we bowled along Piccadilly. Heavy traffic had returned to Trafalgar Square. Only the large quantity of litter in the gutters gave evidence of last night's activities.

'Want me to stop outside Number Ten?' the cabby asked, as he narrowly missed a television truck at the entrance to the street.

'Go right down to the end,' I said, feeling in my pocket for the fare. My natural meanness reasserted itself here and I confined my tip to two bob. It happened to be a shining tenpenny piece. The cabby held it up to the light as if to make sure it was genuine.

'Now that's what I call a fair tip,' he said tossing the coin.

'I hope so.'

'Maybe I could tell you a thing or two. E're, take a look at this,' he said, pointing beside him.

I pushed my head through his window and looked down at a small expensive-looking tape recorder.

'It's a tape recorder,' I said, not over-impressed.

'Right. And what would I use it for?'

'Recording.'

'Right Guv. But don't get me wrong, 'enery 'orsefield ain't no nark. That's for the "bowler boys", the City Brigade,' he said with immense pride.

'How come?' I asked, now curious.

'I take cab loads of 'em from Victoria and Waterloo down to the City every mornin', and I brings 'em back every evenin'.'

'And record what they say,' I said with a smile.

'Correct. You'd be surprised what people 'as to say in the security and comfort of my cab. The wife types it all up every night.'

'You know the fellows with the hot tips? The brokers I mean.'

Here the cabby drew in his breath.

'Ain't you the smart one,' he cried, his eyes shining. 'I been at this game for all of twenty years. Every mornin' and evenin' I carries the same set of city gents, if you see my meanin'.'

'I certainly do. Do your investments pay off?'

'Investments pay off? D'you think I run this old hearse for the purpose of carryin' gentlemen like you? No disrespect you understand.' Here he seemed to break into a sort of silent helpless laughter. 'Invest,' he suddenly roared, when he caught his breath, 'you tell 'is nibs up there that I could buy 'im and 'is party up an' never notice it. Here, Guv, you take this, you might need it some day!'

He spun the tenpenny piece in my direction. Mechanically I caught it. Before I could reply he was gone.

CHAPTER NINE

DOWNING STREET AGAIN

I walked casually back down the street towards Number 10. Pressmen were lounging near the door. With only yards to go one of them spoke to me. I leaped to a defensive position between the two policemen on guard. It hardly seemed possible that it was less than twenty-four hours since my previous visit. The bobbies looked me up and down, which was only natural as they'd been on duty when I'd made my dramatic exit.

'I left some papers here yesterday,' I lied brazenly.

This seemed the simplest way to secure admittance. One of the policemen turned and rang the bell. A few moments later I was inside.

'Gentleman says he left some papers here, yesterday,' said the policeman to the bespectacled fellow who admitted us.

'Dr West?' inquired the attendant. I nodded. 'Ah, the Prime Minister's private secretary would have your papers. If you'll come this way.' A moment later and I was back in the same ante-room.

The door closed leaving me alone with my thoughts, which at this moment were largely concerned with 'enery 'orsefield and with the prospect of his buying up the government.

'Sorry I've been so long, Dr West.' The private

secretary was a young chap, dark, medium build, carefully dressed. He presented no challenge of personality, which I suppose was an important quality in his particular post.

'I'm not sure what papers you left behind,' he went on.

'For the moment let's forget the papers. You heard what was said at the meeting yesterday morning?'

'Of course.'

'Well, my point of view probably seemed very strange.'

'It looks a bit better today, by what I've heard.'

'I certainly think so. My problem is there are some new points which have come to my mind. I happen to think they're important. I think the P.M. should at least know about them. So I was wondering whether you'd be kind enough to tell him?'

'I could hardly . . .' the secretary began.

'I could write it down.'

'Well, Dr West, I appreciate how you feel, but the P.M. has a lot on his mind, especially after last night. He was in the House until early this morning.'

'I hear there were disturbances?'

'I believe so,' said the man, observing me. 'Look,' he continued at length, 'the P.M.'s having breakfast at the moment. If you'd like to wait I'll have a word with him.'

'Thank you.'

The secretary left me once again to commune with the dreadful pictures on the walls. He was back again much sooner than I'd expected with the news that the P.M. had agreed to see me. It struck me as we climbed the stairs that in an odd way the chap was uneasy. It was an impression, not anything he said.

'Ah, Dr West!' exclaimed the P.M., welcoming me to his study, 'we meet again.'

'Yes, sir.'

'Take a seat. I hear you've something on your mind.'

'I hope my ideas yesterday don't look quite as crazy now as they did then,' I said, remaining standing.

'I don't remember saying anything about being crazy. That isn't a word I ever permit myself to use.'

This statement set me off-balance for a moment. 'You know about the elephant and about the trees?'

'Of course. One advantage or disadvantage, I don't know which, of being a politician is that one hears everything.'

'Well, sir, I'm going to take it as a clear fact that we're dealing with the same creature. Both the elephant and the trees.'

'I'll accept that, Dr West.'

'There's been a pattern to the creature. I hadn't realized it until this morning, but I think it's of great importance. The shapes are sequential.'

'Sequential,' murmured the P.M., stuffing his pipe with tobacco until it flowed over the brim of the bowl.

'Yes. It wasn't until Adcock took a fatal fall that the bees appeared. And it wasn't until the bees died that the Pyrenean dogs appeared.'

'How did the bees die?' he asked between sucks on the pipe.

'They were sprayed with insecticide. But they died from lack of oxygen. They were too big.'

'I see, and it wasn't until the dog was trampled that

the white elephant appeared. Quite a creature from the reports I hear.'

'Quite right, sir.'

'And it wasn't until the white elephant was shot up that these damned trees appeared,' the P.M. continued reflectively.

'Now, sir, this next point is extremely important. The military are preparing to chop those trees down, I believe. This is sheer insanity. We've got the creature locked up in the trees. Why let it loose again? Suppose it became a virulent plague?' I added for good measure.

'I'm with you, Dr West. In fact I'm ahead of you,' roared the P.M., blowing smoke like a battleship throwing out a screen. He grabbed hold of a bright red phone on the desk. 'Get me the Minister of Defence. No, get him round here. When! Now! Now this minute, of course.'

He slammed the phone down and puffed. My eyes had started to water and the urge to cough was overwhelming.

'Dr West. You will discover shortly that I am a man of action, a man of intense energy. You were saying?'

'I was going to say exactly what you've already seen, sir,' I said trying to clear my throat. 'We've got the creature immobilized. Maybe we need the military there to protect those trees, not to uproot them.'

'I agree. I agree absolutely. We'll put top class security on them.'

'The point, sir, is that those sequoias are remarkably shallow-rooted. From their height you'd think the roots would go deep, but they don't. It would be extremely dangerous to have too many people trampling around too close to them. It would loosen the soil far too much. Very likely they'd blow down in a high wind. As long as the guard keeps people at a fair distance . . .'

'A fair distance,' repeated the P.M., surrounded by a swirling cloud of blue smoke.

'Fifty to a hundred feet I'd say. But you can get good advice from the people who'd know about it.'

'Anything else?'

'Yes, sir, lightning. With their great height they'd be struck during thunderstorms.'

'Hm. What can we do about that?'

'Fit them with lightning conductors.'

'And what do we do about aircraft?'

'Markers will have to be put around them, and flight paths changed if necessary. With care those trees could stay the way they are for a thousand years.'

'I wish I could get as clear and succinct a statement as that from members of my Cabinet,' nodded the P.M., again blurring my vision with his smoke.

The door must have opened for the secretary suddenly glided past me and handed the P.M. a sheet of paper, whispering urgently in his ear. The Prime Minister jumped to his feet.

'Excuse me a moment, Dr West, a most important matter has arisen. Please stay here, as there's another issue on which I would value your opinion.'

Then he and his secretary were gone, leaving the study door ajar as it happened. I had no doubt the P.M.'s hurried departure was connected with the arrival of the Minister of Defence. It wasn't long before I heard raised voices through the slightly open door. I would challenge the least curious of mortals not to be tempted by the prospect of listening to a Prime Minister bawling out his Minister of Defence. I moved quietly over the thick pile carpet to a position just behind the door. Then with great care I pulled it gently further open. The voices now became audible. With a shock I realized that it wasn't the Minister of Defence at all who had arrived, but a very August Person.

'It may be unusual for me to visit here at this hour or even at all, Prime Minister, but I tell you, Buck Palace simply isn't a place in which to receive anyone at the moment. What, I would like to know, are you going to do about it?'

There was a moment's silence.

'Might I suggest a little patience, Ma'am.'

'Look here, and not to put a fine point on it, the place is as black as hell.'

'Quite so, quite so. I appreciate your concern.'

'What d'you mean "quite so"? You make it sound as though you'd arranged it all.'

'Ma'am, even a Prime Minister can't make trees grow to order, to a height of three hundred feet in a single night.'

'Then if you can't, who can?'

This appeared to silence the P.M.

'After outseeing more Prime Ministers than I would care to name I am of the persuasion that it is time to put my foot firmly and squarely down,' went on the August Person. It seemed an eternity before the P.M. responded. I felt sure the word 'outsee' had shaken him.

'Let us proceed with caution and calm. Rome wasn't built in a day.'

'No, but those trees were. Who did it, that's what I'd like to know. The flower man at the B.B.C.?'

'I must be frank with you, Ma'am. We don't know.'

'But it is the business of my Government to know.'

'All I need is a little time, a little caution . . .'

'A little fiddle-di-dee. Take each tree to be a right cylinder, diameter six feet, length three hundred feet, and you will find each one to have a volume of some eight thousand five hundred cubic feet.'

'Doubtless, Ma'am. Doubtless.'

'At a density comparable to water,' went on the August Person relentlessly, 'you will find each tree to have a mass of some two hundred tons.'

'Doubtless . . .' I heard the P.M. say again.

'Will you please stop saying that. Two hundred tons for each tree means ten thousand tons for a hundred trees. Ten thousand tons of wood, in an esoteric form, transported into the Palace grounds in the middle of the night! And you say you don't know!'

'There's more to it than meets the eye, Ma'am.'

'Inside the Palace nothing meets the eye. The place is as black as the hole of Calcutta.'

'With which our forefathers dealt magnificently.'

There was another long pause, from which I deduced it was the turn of the August Person to be stumped. The attack was then resumed from a new direction.

'What is this I hear about a white elephant, Mr Prime Minister?'

'A white elephant!'

'I hear a white elephant took over most of London

last night and went rah-rah-rahing through the streets with a motley collection of followers!'

'There were some disturbances, I understand.'

'It is widely believed that the elephant forced its way into the Commons and entered the Chamber while you yourself were speaking.'

'A grotesque and monstrous fabrication,' erupted the P.M., his voice rising.

'I would have thought it hardly necessary to remind you, of all people, Mr Prime Minister, that it is not the truth in politics which matters. It is what is believed to be the truth.'

'I shall take all necessary steps to scotch this wild and ugly rumour.'

'Far be it from me to advise you on what is properly your own business, but you cannot expect people to believe that those trees were the work of the flower man at the B.B.C. and for them not to believe the story of the white elephant in the House. For all practical purposes, the elephant did invade the Chamber last night. The sooner you get that into your head the better.'

'It's quite preposterous, Ma'am.'

'Preposterous or not, I shall expect a full report on the incident.'

'Report!' the P.M.'s voice was squeaky now.

'This is precisely the sort of situation that could provoke a constitutional crisis. I must have a working brief, or would you prefer me to speak freely?' This was followed by an extremely long pause.

'Ma'am,' began the P.M., slowly and deliberately, 'I must speak frankly. I did not wish to alarm you, we did not wish to alarm you, your government did not wish to alarm you, but those trees are the work of . . .'

'Invaders from outer space,' concluded the August Person.

'Yes, from outer space,' admitted the P.M.

'Then I have decided on a pent-house, a small manageable pent-house.'

'What has a pent-house to do with it?'

'I have decided to change my residence. From an unmanageable Palace to a manageable pent-house.'

'Quite impossible.'

'It is just as impossible to stay where I am, with a hundred invaders from outer space towering over my head. My people would not permit such an outrage. They would tear you and your government limb from limb.'

'This is not a matter on which I can give a ready answer. It raises serious problems.'

'Such as?'

'Such as the Carriage with its magnificent horses, so necessary on great days of state. How should we cope with that I wonder?'

'I do not number persons of rude speech among my acquaintances, but if I did they would undoubtedly answer by advising you to stuff it.'

'Ma'am!'

'I am merely bringing to your notice the temper of a certain section of my people.'

'I will appoint a committee immediately . . .'

'No committee, never. Remember Mr Prime Minister, you are a man of action.'

'I admit, Ma'am, that you have an important point there. I shall attend to the matter with remarkable dispatch!'

'And remember this—I said a manageable pent-house, not a mansion pent-house.'

'The difference is instantly clear to me.'

'Good, then we can move on to a different issue. With my foot firmly and squarely on the ground . . .'

My ears, strained to catch this conversation, were sensitive to an approaching footfall. I took a step back from the door, glanced round and made for the bookcase.

'I thought you'd like this, sir,' said a man in a white coat carrying a tray.

'Thank you, that's very kind.' I turned from the bookcase. The man nodded and withdrew, closing the door firmly behind him. I wondered about reopening it, but the sudden arrival of the attendant had made me sensitive to the danger of being caught eavesdropping. I examined the tray—coffee.

I was through two cups of it and starting a third when I heard the door click behind me and saw that the P.M. had returned.

'A-ha! The cares of State weigh heavily on my shoulders,' he cried, puffing like a squadron of ships. 'It's fortunate indeed that I am a man of intense energy, Dr West.'

'Can I pour you a cup of coffee?' I said standing up.

'No, hate the stuff, but help yourself.'

I automatically topped up my cup.

'Dr West, I have a problem of immense magnitude on my mind.'

'That's certainly true, sir.'

'Wait 'til you've heard what I have to tell you. I suppose you recall the Russo-Chinese troubles of last winter?'

'Yes, there was fighting I remember, across some frozen river or other.'

'The Amur River, at Dzhalinda. Bitter fighting. Relations were exceedingly grave.'

'I understand something . . .' I began, but the P.M. swept relentlessly along.

'The freezing of the river in winter creates a border more than a thousand miles long across which you can merely walk from one country to another.'

'Which makes border politics worse in winter I suppose.'

'Which makes it worse in winter. So you'd expect things to improve with the spring thaw—eh?'

'I haven't seen any reports recently,' I said, perplexed by the direction of the conversation.

'Dr West, you're not with me. It isn't just the fighting dying down with the spring thaw. Over the past few months there has been a sudden, dramatic and quite unexpected improvement in the relations between Russia and China.'

'Why should this worry you, Prime Minister?'

'The emphasis is on dramatic.'

'I suppose if you're hoping to set the Russians and Chinese off against each other . . .'

'I still say the emphasis is on the word dramatic. Look. I'll put it another way. Was the invasion confined to this country?'

'From outer space, you mean?'

'Yes, yes,' cried the P.M. now becoming excited. I began to grasp what he was suggesting.

'I don't see why it should have been,' I said, 'after all, the thing came in here through Heathrow Airport.'

'Just so. It came in from outside. Like the black plague rats of times gone by.'

'From the United States?'

'Which suggests something might be happening in America.'

'And possibly in both Russia and China,' I concluded triumphantly.

'Now you're with me, Dr West!' The P.M. started to relight his pipe.

'I should have seen this before.'

'Not at all, Dr West. It would have been disappointing if every idea had come from you. I was in Moscow in March, as you may remember. There was nothing bad enough that the Russians could say about the Chinese at that time.'

'It hadn't really started here—in March.'

'The question we have to ask ourselves . . .'

'Is whether the creatures have captured the Soviet and Chinese governments. If they have, then perhaps they wouldn't want to fight each other,' I again concluded triumphantly.

The P.M. puffed hard on his pipe, staring out into space. All kinds of thoughts raced through my mind. There was the American withdrawal from South-East Asia, followed by the friendly overtures between Russia and China. Even the Arabs and the Israelis had started talking to each other.

'Nine hundred million people in Russia and China. Almost a third of all the people on Earth. It boggles the imagination,' the P.M. muttered.

'It may not be as bad as you think. After all, friendly relations don't amount to proof,' I offered consolingly.

'Maybe not, but I see the situation in an extremely sinister light.'

He puffed away at his pipe for some time and then pressed what I took to be a bell and stood up. Taking the cue, I jumped to my feet also.

'I expect we'll meet again, Dr West. It's been useful talking to you, but don't make a habit of dropping in. Write if you have anything further to say.'

I watched him for a moment, trying to fathom a sudden change in his voice. The door opened and the private secretary came in.

'Henry, could you see Dr West out? I don't wish to be disturbed for the rest of the morning. I've got important Cabinet papers to read.'

So there I was, on my way downstairs, past the pictures again. I couldn't remember all these politicians from the past but I felt they must know me by now.

'You didn't have a coat?'

'No.'

'I wonder if I could have a word with you, Dr West, in private?' The secretary was obviously yielding to a sudden impulse.

There was nobody in the ante-room, so I was back in there for the third time. Henry, the secretary, walked hesitatingly over to a large window.

'Something is very wrong with the Prime Minister,' he blurted out.

'Wrong?' I asked.

'It's really in small things, but he's changed.'

'Has he seen the doctor? The strain of the last few days coming on top of everything else may be getting him down.'

'I wondered about that, but he's really very fit.'

'What kind of changes?' I asked.

'Well, did he say anything to you about being a man of intense energy?'

'Yes, as a matter of fact he did.'

'How many times?'

'Twice or maybe three times, I can't remember.'

'Well, it's a sort of mannerism with him. He used to come out with it two or three times a week. To let off steam. Now he's saying it about twenty times a day.'

'Other mannerisms as well?'

'Yes, but mostly things an outsider wouldn't notice. Except for the smoking. That's got completely out of hand.'

I cursed myself for sheer imbecility. What an appalling pumpkin I'd been. I gripped the secretary fiercely by the arm and propelled him upstairs in front of me. We took the stairs two at a time, and strode along to the P.M.'s study.

'Announce me,' I said, pushing Henry towards the closed door. Extremely quietly he poked his head round the door and whispered that I was back. I gave the P.M. no time to react. I went in past the secretary, indicated that he should withdraw, and shut the door. The P.M. was sitting there like a fuming Buddha. There were no Cabinet papers at all in front of him.

'R. A. Adcock,' I said as I reached the edge of the desk.

He made no immediate response but continued to puff out huge clouds of swirling smoke.

CHAPTER TEN

CONFRONTATION

'Dr West, I am severely disappointed in you,' were
the first words.

'I was exceedingly stupid.'

'I shall not quarrel with that judgment. When you
arrived here first thing this morning I fully expected
you had already reached your present conclusion.'

'Which was why you agreed to see me?'

'It was. But even after I gave you hint after hint
you still sat there like a block of wood.'

'I went wrong with the sequential idea. I couldn't
get it out of my head that one shape had to follow
another.'

'And what shape do you see now?'

I forbore to tell him an exceedingly sinister one.
'I see the elephant and the trees are a complete blind
alley. To make us think we've got you locked away.
Very clever.'

'To you, yes. To me, no.'

'You made a switch between the P.M. and the
Pyrenean dog. You arranged the air attack on the
elephant. You arranged the blackout. Who better
placed than you, sitting there in the Prime Minister's
shoes. Exploding your own elephant. Very subtle.'

To this there was no response.

'So it's the real P.M. who is locked up in those trees.'

The Buddha shook his head. Another idea flashed through my mind:

'Ah! His Chief Scientific Adviser!'

'Dr West, you have an uncanny knack of arriving at the truth.'

I pondered the situation for a while, until he continued:

'Which of course was why I singled you out in the first place.'

'Singled me out?'

'Hasn't it occurred to you that you always happen to be around whenever anything important happens?'

'As a matter of fact, yes it has; I've been worried by it to the point of questioning my own sanity.'

'There's an odd psychic streak in you, Dr West. What was it may I ask that finally aroused your suspicions.'

'The smoking. You're overdoing it.'

'Thank god for that.'

Here he went without expression to the window and flung the pipe in the direction of Horse Guards Parade.

'But where *is* the real P.M.?'

'Remember the court case. Remember the bank-teller. Work it out from there.'

I had a vague idea of what he meant.

'You've come a long way since the court case.'

'Indeed. I am now in what you might call an impregnable position.'

'Except your party could be thrown out of office.'

'So it could. But why would that make any difference to me?'

'I suppose not.' I saw that if he could replace one P.M. he could replace another. To him there really wasn't any difference, and, if the truth be admitted, to the rest of us as well.

'I could speak out against you.'

'In the newspapers?'

'Yes.'

'Do you think anybody would believe you?'

'After the elephant and the trees, yes.'

'Possibly. But I wonder if you have any conception of how very easy it would be for me to prevent you from taking such a step.'

There was something completely impassive about the creature who now occupied the Prime Minister's shape. The multiplicity of gaucheries that had distinguished R. A. Adcock in court were gone. But the withdrawn quality was the same.

'To put it in terms of mediaeval witchery, you could change me into the smallest mouse!'

'Yes, or to be more dignified, I could change you into the tallest tree.'

'Together with your scientific adviser.'

'Advisers, *and* Science policy and Research Councils.'

'It would be a somewhat cowardly solution to your problem.'

'I am inclined to agree with you. On the whole I suggest you simply give me your word to keep silent.'

'I could.'

Here I remembered R.A.Adcock's strange pre-occupation in court with the truth.

'It would be the simplest way. I suggest you return to your home, which is where by the way?'

'Cambridge.'

'You give me your word?'

'Yes.'

'It is possible that I shall communicate with you further.'

Here he relapsed into a trance. I watched for as long as ten minutes I suppose. Then suddenly with a violent start he half lifted himself out of the chair and said:

'Ah-ha, Dr West! I thought I'd seen the last of you. When I consider the number of my visitors and the extent of my commitments, it is indeed fortunate that I am a man of intense energy. Now where the devil is my pipe?'

'I was just going, Prime Minister. I wonder if I might spend a few moments on the way out examining your pictures?'

'If you could interest a gang of thieves in 'em I'd be grateful. Now where in the name of invaders from outer space is my pipe?'

I slipped away from the study leaving him searching with concentrated fury. It was clear now just where the P.M. was locked. Fantastically enough, inside himself. For the most part, it was still the P.M. expressing himself, but then in a flash the intelligence of R.A. Adcock could assume control. At such times the P.M. had no knowledge of what was going on just as the wretched teller in Lewisham had had no idea of what took place when R. A. Adcock, in his shape, robbed the bank. To the man Sheppard it had seemed like a loss of memory, just as the P.M. had no memory now of tossing his pipe so dramatically into Horse Guards Parade.

The private secretary was waiting anxiously.

'It's a case of overstrain,' I lied.

'But . . .'

'I had a word with him about the smoking.'

'Did he chew you out?'

'Not at all. He threw his pipe away.'

'Threw his pipe away!'

'Into Horse Guards Parade.'

'What!'

'He's regretting it now. If you were to slip outside and find it, I think he'd be grateful.'

'You're joking, Dr West.'

'No, dead serious.'

'Then I'll go along right away.'

'Before you do, let me give you a tip.'

'Yes?'

'Don't try to stop him when he's smoking naturally. But when he starts the Buddha act . . .'

'I know exactly what you mean.'

'Emitting great clouds . . .'

'. . . like a volcano.'

'Have a word with him then.'

'I will.'

'See if you can find the pipe. But before you go, might I pop into the Cabinet room for a moment?'

'It's a bit unusual, but I don't see why not. It's empty at the moment.'

He showed me in, and then left hurriedly on his

errand of retrieval. I shut the door, sitting in what I judged to be the same chair as before. I looked across to where the man with the flying hair had sat. His leaves now would be flying in the wind. It was uncannily like the old story of Daphne and Apollo, except that Daphne had been a good-looking piece. So it was with all of them. There they were clustered around the Palace, sighing in the wind, advising mankind towards a less frenzied, more dignified way of life. Which was probably better advice than they'd ever given before.

With a slight shock, I noticed from the clock on the wall that it was exactly twenty-four hours since I'd begun my ill-fated speech. I glanced around the empty room for the last time and took my leave.

My exit was quiet today. There were still the inevitable TV chaps, trailing wires all over the place, waiting for the next trade union delegation.

'Would you tell me what's going on, sir?'

'Issues of incredible magnitude are being discussed.'

This took the chap aback. The whole of his training had been concerned with the technique of interviewing shifty and evasive customers.

'What issues, sir?' was all he could manage.

'A mission of vast scientific import is being organized.'

I seemed to have picked up the political gib-gab.

'What might that be?'

'The future is at stake of the giant tortoises of the Seychelles Islands.'

This provided a pause long enough for me to make my escape.

Once again I walked briskly along Whitehall but

this time with a sense of acute anticlimax. Nothing would be so good ever again. I ought of course to have been overwhelmed by sinister foreboding. It was clear the aliens from outer space had taken over now, almost without a shot being fired. But oddly enough this hardly concerned me at all. It was the thought that the episode of R. A. Adcock in court, the episode of the white elephant, the thought that they were over and finished with, that strangely depressed me. There was nothing to do but go home. My first notion was to take a taxi to Liverpool Street, but even the cabby wouldn't match up to 'enery 'orsefield.

CHAPTER ELEVEN

CLIMAX

The following morning, back in Cambridge, I tried to contact several of my colleagues at the laboratory but without much success. Either they weren't answering their phones or they were away. I roamed around the house for several hours before eventually deciding to do something constructive. It soon became a clear objective to set everything down on paper, just as it had happened, before I began to forget what had been said. I still remembered vividly expressions on faces and tones of voice. For the next few days I wrote furiously.

To understand the behaviour of the news media at this time it is necessary to appreciate a very critical point. Physicists would describe most of what happens in everyday life as 'noise'. This is best explained by saying that 'noise' consists of activity without information content. 'Signal' consists of genuine information. A signal-to-noise problem in physics consists in digging out genuine information from activity without content.

With this understood, it is possible to assess what goes on in the press and in our universities. The protagonists of studies in the humanities fail to appreciate the extent to which their problems are of the signal-to-noise kind, difficult problems too, often with little signal. Instead of separating the noise—throwing it away as the physicists do—they spend their energies chasing through every detail of the darned stuff. Students of history do this with ferocious concentration, spending year after year studying their 'period' as they call it. Students of sociology might indeed be described as the ultimate students of noise, literally and figuratively. Instead of putting a smart stop to this nonsense, universities are proceeding energetically to expand it. The predictable consequence is bedlam.

The news media are a step farther in the same wrong direction. Instead of merely pursuing noise for its own sake as the universities do, they deliberately expend their best efforts on misidentifying it. An elaborate pretence is set up whereby issues of no consequence are puffed up until they distract us all from understanding the simplest aspects of life.

It is not hard therefore to understand why at this time the press set up a great uproar and fuss, and why the press was largely without relevance to the activities of R. A. Adcock. A big production was made out of my chance remark about the Seychelles Islands. By about midweek it appeared that a plane full of the country's top scientists had gone astray somewhere in the Indian Ocean. A leader in *The Times* thundered against the 'sheer folly' of concentrating so much valuable brain power together under vulnerable circumstances, quite failing to realize that the brains were still together—whispering in the wind, high above Green Park.

One electrifying peak of signal did come through however. The U.S. President was on his way to the U.K. So was the President of the U.S.S.R. So astonishingly enough was the great Chairman Mao. This was a real body blow to the Common Marketeers, since it was clear to everyone that if Britain had been 'in' Europe the meeting would inevitably have taken place in Paris.

My sense of anticlimax had given way now to a resigned feeling that the whole affair had somehow slipped away from me. From being in the very eye of the hurricane I was experiencing an enforced leave. I suppose this is the way many people feel after they've retired. So you can imagine my surprise when, returning from an afternoon walk, I found a government messenger waiting on my doorstep. He handed me a large envelope which I instantly slit open:

THE PRIME MINISTER

Requests the honour of the company of Dr Archibald John West at a meeting to be held at Chequers on Sunday 24 June at
11 a.m.
10.45 a.m. for 11 a.m.
Coffee will be served.

'Can you take a reply?' I asked after reading it twice.

'Yes, sir. If you're going to attend, I'm to tell you that a car will be here at a quarter to eight tomorrow morning.'

'I'll be ready.'

'Very good, sir,' said the messenger with a stiffening of his body. I half expected a click of the heels and a bit of hand waving, but the fellow just turned and left.

I suddenly realized that it must be Saturday. I'd lost count of the days of the week in the urgency of my writings. The rest of the day was spent in bringing my manuscript up to date.

In the car the following morning I thought over the situation for perhaps the tenth time. I remembered the true R. A. Adcock had said we might see each other again. Was this a summons from him or was it a maverick invitation from the P.M.? For the tenth time I decided this question couldn't be answered until we reached Chequers.

I tried to close my mind to unprofitable speculation by taking in the country scene. Our route led through those country lanes and by-ways which are mostly forgotten in the rush to speed quickly from A to B. Trees and flowers bloomed in profusion, cattle grazed lazily in passing fields, and the road was alive with birds playing their own version of Russian roulette. It was the kind of day that reminded me of an American girl's remark, 'In England in the spring it seems as if the whole world is having a baby.'

Such a thought made strange contrast to the meeting ahead of me. Four men controlling a half of the world's population. Four men, themselves prisoners in the hands of an invader from outer space. The strangest thing of all was my own part in it. Instinctively I felt that a powerful trick lay somewhere in my hands, if only I could discover it. I'd never thought of myself as psychic but now I began to suspect it might be so. At all events I was entirely convinced that the affair was working itself to an unexpected climax.

I was so wrapped up in these ideas that I didn't realize we were at our destination until the car turned into a gateway. From outside the main door I was escorted with little ceremony through various rooms and corridors until I found myself on a wide lawn. Immediately I noticed a shining structure about fifteen feet across and three to four high on the far side of the lawn. Walking towards it, I saw it was a splendid Carousel, constructed of silver. Distinctive use had been made of semi-precious stones. Truly a most splendid carousel. An electric cable had been laid to it from the house. I found a switch and was quite unable to resist pressing it. The enormous toy started to rotate. As the platform picked up speed, human figures moved and a musical box played Yankee Doodle, from which I deduced that this carousel must be a gift from the American President to his host.

The tonal quality of the musical box suggested times long gone-by, but curiously enough the figures were in modern dress. I waited for the machinery to run down, I waited for the wistful sagging of pitch from the musical box. Then I realized that, being electrically driven, it would never run down. As the figures continued to revolve I could hear birds in the garden singing above the music, and over the whole scene came the rich aroma of heavily scented old-fashioned shrub roses.

I was startled by an attendant, not the same one as before, appearing suddenly behind me.

'They're waiting for you, sir,' he said.

Hurriedly I switched off the electric supply. The music died instantly. As I followed the attendant to the house the thought struck me that this chap in front of me was really no different from the figures I'd just been watching. In fact all of us were just going round and round on the same journey, a journey from birth to death, one generation after another.

Inside the house again we stopped at a door. The attendant knocked and then ushered me into a moderately large room. Books lined the walls. Carpets and curtains would be effective sound dampeners. Easy to talk here, I thought.

'Ah, Dr West! Let me welcome you once more. Here let me make the introductions. The President of the U.S.S.R.'

We shook hands.

'The President of the United States of America.'

We shook hands.

'Chairman Mao.'

Unable to reach Chairman Mao for a handshake I made a half bow. The large moon face grimaced back at me. We were standing near a table bearing a large tumbler of clear liquid, which Mao raised and quaffed in reply to the introduction. By its quantity and from the speed with which he drank the stuff I took it to be water.

'You may wonder why you are here, Dr West?' said the P.M.

'That's quite correct, sir,' I said in as matter of fact a tone as I could manage.

'You are here because I had the forethought to realize we might need a secretary,' he said, turning to the others. 'I take it none of you gentlemen wishes to take down the minutes?'

Both Presidents shook their heads and Chairman

Mao raised his hands, palms towards me, one hand on each side of his face. Then he drank another tumbler of water, which he poured from a large jug.

'Before we begin I take it you'd like a refill of that pitcher?' noted the P.M., pressing a service button.

Mao once again lifted his glass in assent.

'I need only add,' continued the P.M., 'that Dr West is the one person who fully understands the true position, and that his discretion is such that anything we say will stay within the walls of this room.'

There was a knock and an attendant, the first attendant, the one who had shown me out on to the lawn, came in carrying a second truly vast pitcher which he set down in front of Mao.

When the attendant had withdrawn we all sat down at a rectangular table. The P.M. took the Chairman's position at one end. I took the other end, equipped now with a large pad. On my right sat the President of the U.S., on my left the President of the U.S.S.R. together with Chairman Mao. It struck me as being a bit like the scrimmage position in American football, with the P.M. and me as referees, and with the President of the U.S. one man short.

'The first topic on our agenda, gentlemen, is the question of spheres of influence,' announced the P.M.

Dutifully I wrote *Spheres of Influence* at the top of my pad, meanwhile thinking that whatever agenda there might be must be in the P.M.'s head, for there was no sheet of paper in front of him, or indeed before any of the others.

Instead of continuing, the P.M. again pressed his service button. We all waited. A moment later in came the first attendant carrying a tray of cups and two large jugs of coffee. I was wondering why he couldn't have brought in the coffee together with Mao's water when the second attendant—the one who had fetched me from the lawn—followed with a second tray which he laid in the middle of the rectangular table. On this second tray was a very large cake, two to three feet across and about four inches thick. The cake was a yellow sponge with a layer of jam in the middle, the sort I'm quite fond of.

The cake was already cut out into sectors, each of which had lettering on top. One was marked AFRICA, another INDIA, S. AMERICA, MIDDLE EAST. . . . The President of the U.S. immediately moved to pick up the piece marked VIETNAM. Before he could do so, however, both Mao and the President of the U.S.S.R. crashed their fists down on this particular sector.

'It's ruined,' I cried out, indignantly, looking at the flattened mass of crumbs.

'Precisely so,' nodded the P.M., a well-satisfied smirk on his face. 'Take that down,' he instructed me.

I wrote a few words. Then a thought struck me. I remembered the 'coffee will be served' on the P.M.'s invitation card. I'd expected to be meeting creatures not of the Earth but I'd hardly guessed it could be anything quite like this. Yet I was beginning to see, still rather vaguely, some structure in what was going on.

'Pour yourself coffee,' the P.M. further instructed me.

'Shall I pour for everyone?' I asked.

'The rest of us will not be drinking, except Mao and he prefers water.'

Mao evidently did prefer water, for the enormous pitcher was already half empty. I poured myself a cup.

'Pour several,' the P.M. instructed yet again.

Since I usually drink three cups I poured three and then took them all to my end of the table.

'Spheres of influence,' went on the Prime Minister. 'What have you got to say, Mr President of the U.S.S.R.?'

'In my country,' the President of U.S.S.R. began, 'we have a proverb.' He stopped and held up his right hand in an oratorical gesture. I lifted my pen to take down the proverb. The Russian President then screwed up his nose, curled his lip and leant over towards the American President.

'He who lives among dogs must learn to pant,' he declaimed.

Then the Russian President began a rapid hah-hah-hah-hah-haing directly up into the American President's face.

'O.K., Fido,' responded the American President.

'Gentlemen, gentlemen!' boomed the P.M. 'Let us remember that the eyes of the world are turned towards us. Let us seize this great opportunity with both hands.' For a moment it looked as though seizing each other with both hands would be exactly what the two Presidents would do, especially when the American lifted both arms high above the head in his election-winning imitation of the eagle.

'Let us display a proper sense of history,' shouted the P.M. despairingly. The situation was saved by Mao, who announced in a lilting sing-song voice,

'History is a paper tiger.'

This stopped us all dead in our tracks.

'What was that, Mao?' asked the P.M.

For answer Mao smoothly drank another pint of water—it seemed to go down without the larynx moving. Then the moon face nodded for a moment. 'History is a paper tiger,' he repeated.

'I don't dig that,' exclaimed the President of the U.S.

The moon face expanded still further,

'The atom bomb is a paper tiger,' it said.

'I don't dig that either.'

'We shall dig your grave,' bellowed the Russian. 'We shall bury capitalism.'

Mao rocked backward and forward in his chair, 'Capitalism is a paper tiger,' he crooned. 'Russia is a paper tiger,' he added for good measure.

'Before this gets out of hand, Mao,' interrupted the P.M., hastily, 'I think we'd better check up on these thoughts of yours.'

The Prime Minister jumped from his seat to the bookcase. A moment later he was back at the table brandishing a small book bound in a red cover.

'Ah—yes,' said he. 'The thoughts of our respected comrade here on my right. Comprehensively indexed —which is fortunate, to say the least. Now what do we want—paper tigers—paper tigers. Here we are: "paper tigers, fascist; paper tigers, capitalist." Yes our friend said that all right, "paper tigers, iron; paper tigers, bean curd." Now I wonder what that could mean. Oh—ho, what have we here, "paper tigers, atom bomb". There we are, Mao did say it after all.'

Mao continued his rocking. 'The atom bomb is a paper tiger,' he averred benignly.

'I still don't dig it,' said the American President. 'But I'd like to see it all the same.'

The P.M. handed over the little red book to the President of the U.S. After studying it for a couple of minutes, the President shook his head in a puzzled way. 'That's what it says, so I suppose it must be right,' he admitted.

In triumph Mao lifted the enormous pitcher and drank what was left of the water. This time I heard the gurgle as it went down.

'Perhaps I should explain, Dr West,' interposed the P.M. 'Chairman Mao became addicted to shipping vast quantities of water during his fantastic and epoch-making swims.'

As if to add weight to this explanation, Mao banged the pitcher on the table with an enormous thump.

'Another—eh?' asked the P.M.

Mao nodded in dazed fashion. I could hardly believe Mao could become drunk on water, but this was certainly what it looked like.

The American President waited until the attendant had refilled Mao's pitcher and had left the room. Then he asked of the Russian President, 'How many paper tigers you got, Russki?'

'Are you taking all this down, Dr West?'

'I'm doing my best, Prime Minister.'

To my surprise the P.M. then spoke in Russian, presumably translating the question about paper tigers, which the President of the U.S.S.R. clearly had not understood at first. For answer, the Russian eventually took a sheaf of papers from his inside pocket. He thumbed slowly through them at quite painful length.

'One thousand and three,' he said at last. 'Of bombs ...'

'Paper tigers,' grunted the American, 'I asked about paper tigers, didn't I?'

Mao nodded rhythmically.

'Of bombs with plutonium warheads,' went on the Russian relentlessly, 'one hundred and five. Of bombs with lithium, one hundred and nine. Of bombs—oh—ha-ha—oh-oh—oh-ha-ho—of bombs ...' The President of the U.S.S.R. lapsed into silent laughter. We waited, watching him shake.

'One thousand and three,' he suddenly yelled in ecstasy.

The American President twitched his thumbs at me. Divining that he wanted the pad I pushed it towards him. He took my pen and figured for a while. 'I make that a real good overkill,' he said patronizingly.

'You've got what our think-tank wizbos call an over-kill factor, maybe a little shy of two-and-a-half. Now me, I've got an overkill factor rather better than four.'

The Russian blinked.

'So what it comes down to is this,' concluded the American triumphantly, 'my paper tigers can eat your paper tigers any time of the day.'

'I hope you are getting all this down, Dr West.'

I muttered something and retrieved my pen and the pad. Throughout this Mad Hatter scene—I even had three cups in front of me—I'd been hard at thought. There was a new relationship here between Adcock and the humans under his control. At Downing Street I'd either talked to the P.M. himself or to Adcock, never to a mixture of the two. But here, while I was dealing with Adcock all right, he was somehow letting the human emotions come through. He was forcing the emotions of the two Presidents, of Mao, and of the Prime Minister into a scenario of his own choosing, a scenario reflecting Adcock's own peculiar extraterrestrial sense of humour. The remarkable thing was, absurd as it might be, this charade portrayed the state of world politics pretty accurately. In only a few moments Adcock had demonstrated an unanswerable case to show why he should himself take control of the world. To leave things to these insane human creatures was plainly impossible.

'I think you've taken the farce far enough,' I said.

'I beg your pardon, Dr West.'

'I said you've taken the farce far enough, much as you might be enjoying it, Mr Adcock.'

'I have been waiting for a response from you for some time.' As he said this the Prime Minister instantly reverted to the trancelike state which I had come to associate with Adcock. Instantly too, the other three assumed the same condition. There were four humans but only one creature from outside the Earth.

'Let your remarks be of relevance,' was the cold admonition.

'I can assure you of relevance,' I said with more assurance than I felt. The sudden switch from farce to grim coldness also unnerved me. We humans use humour as a relief from tension. A jolly chap, a humorous guy, is not supposed in our human convention to be severe. He's supposed to be relaxed, easy going. In other words our humour mixes with other qualities. With Adcock it seemed that humour stood apart from other qualities. Indeed it seemed as if humour had to be enacted in a physical way, according to a prescribed scenario—the kind of thing I'd just been witnessing.

'I shall proceed from the particular to the general,' I began. 'In this country we have several levels of decision-making, half a dozen maybe. Let us set the Cabinet at the highest level, number one.'

Four pairs of eyes stared unwinkingly at me.

'For myself,' I went on, 'I have experience of the lower levels, shall we say three, four, five and six. My experience is that decision-making weakens, not as one goes downwards, but the reverse, going upwards. Almost all effective decisions are taken at levels six and five. They only go upwards from there for ratification.'

'They can be stopped at the higher levels,' was the toneless comment. It made no difference that only the Prime Minister spoke, for they were now all the same creature.

'Very rarely, because the higher levels are much less well informed about technical details than the lower levels. By the time an issue moves from stage five to stage three, shall we say, the case for it or against it has been built up in such a watertight form that stage three is reduced perforce to the function of a rubber stamp. Which of course means that stage three plays no real role at all.'

'What do you deduce from all this?'

'The effect I'm talking about exists progressively all the way from stage six to stage three. I don't know from actual experience what happens at stages two and one, but it hardly seems conceivable that any marked reversal can take place. I am confident this progressive weakening of true decision-making continues all the way up the ladder, right from bottom to top.'

'These are wounding words, Dr West. Perhaps I can assure you the Cabinet is constantly making controversial and important decisions,' said the P.M. after a moment's thought. The other three sat like graven images. Mao had not touched a drop of water since assuming the trance state.

'There's a sense in which I've no doubt you're right. The most obvious example is the Law, because often enough you can actually observe the different levels at work on the same case. Sensible clear-cut issues are all decided in the lower courts. Those that go to the higher courts on appeal are said to be the difficult cases, but the word difficult is wrong. The correct word is "undecideable". It is only the undecideable cases that ever reach the highest courts. What actually happens then is that a decision is made by a random process.'

'A random process?'

'Certainly. The random thoughts of the Judges. The brains of the Judges act as random number generators. If, let us say, the random number comes up even, Appellant A wins. If the random number comes up odd, Appellant B wins.'

'This is not dignified talk, Dr West.'

'Dignity plays quite a part in it though. The dignity of the Law must be maintained at all costs. Dignity demands that common people shall remain unaware of the fact that the highest court serves only the purpose of tossing a coin. Since the situation would instantly be exposed if it were possible to try similar cases several times, the random numbers coming up

133

sometimes odd sometimes even, it has to be a basic principle of law that undecideable cases are never tried twice. The only way to arrange for this to be so is to adopt an automatic procedure whereby subsequent cases are forced into following the decision arrived at in the first instance. This is known as the Doctrine of Precedent. This is why lawyers are for ever looking up fat reference books, to see which way the penny fell the first time.'

'Which is leading us where?'

'Back to the Cabinet, or to the Senate, or to any so-called seat of power, and to the conclusion that its function . . .'

'Is merely to toss a coin?'

'It makes decisions only on issues that are undecideable.'

'What are you suggesting, that the Cabinet in fact has no power?'

'Not necessarily. Even decisions taken by the tossing of a coin can have far-reaching consequences. What I am suggesting is that the power you have so ingeniously contrived for yourself, Mr Adcock, is not at root a very satisfactory form of power.'

'Hard words, Dr West.'

'I'm afraid there's more to come. If I may gild the lily a bit, this is exactly why one political party always turns out to be pretty much like any other political party. Once in office the story is always the same.'

Suddenly the U.S. President stood up. 'I'm going outside,' he muttered, 'to contemplate a symbol of our national heritage.'

Then the President of the U.S.S.R. stood up and

nodded. 'I also will leave and play with the Carousel.'

Mao quickly put his hands to his mouth, as if to hold back the flood, and raced for the door.

'Now those gentlemen have left us we can come down to fundamental issues,' I said, once the door was shut again.

'Now those gentlemen have left?'

'Your sense of humour does not escape me, Mr Adcock.'

Then the creature relapsed again into a trance. It was more unnerving than ever to go on talking, since I had no idea now whether I was being heard or not.

'I've got a broad picture of life on this planet. In a straightforward way I see plant life as the starting point. Then animals begin to live on plants, then animals live on each other. At last one animal, we humans, managed to dominate all the others and even to dominate the Earth itself to some extent. At this point the stage became set for a new big step, which I think is where you come into the picture. You arrive here from somewhere outside our planet, with the idea of fastening yourself onto us humans, in much the same way that we fasten ourselves onto the other animals here. They don't understand what we are doing and we don't understand how you perform your conjuring tricks.

'You arrived here from somewhere and you thought it all dead easy. You only had to capture the leaders of a few powerful countries. The U.S. and U.S.S.R., the main industrial nations, China with the most people, and a few more. Then you had it all made. But now, with a real shock, you find you haven't got it made. Capturing the leaders only gives you the status of a croupier at the human roulette wheel. Which I suppose is the idea of the Carousel. You've seen the point. Outwardly you may seem powerful but inwardly you're just a pack of cards,' I said, putting a hand on Mao's *Thoughts*. Flicking through the pages made a sound rather like a pack of cards being shuffled.

There was still no response. The creature sat like a sphinx. So I got up.

'I'm glad I'm not in your shoes, Mr Adcock,' I said, and left.

Nobody tried to stop me. The car was waiting. The drive back to Cambridge took longer on the return journey, partly because the slow Sunday traffic was denser at this later hour, and partly because the driver deviated once or twice from the best route. We reached my front door about mid-afternoon. I thanked the driver and watched him for a moment while he turned the car. I pushed the key into the lock. With the door open I stood on the threshold. The smell of newly mown grass floated through the air, reminding me of the old-fashioned roses and the Carousel. Although the day was fine and sunny, something about the darkened hallway in front of me made my step heavy.

My mouth became dry. For the second time during the whole affair I was badly frightened. The first time was after the Candlemas Feast at Jesus. The same intense fear had struck me then, and at exactly the same place—my hallway. With a flash of perception I saw my reaction then was not related at all to that occasion but was a premonition of my present situation.

I knew with startling clarity that I should instantly retrace my footsteps and leave the house.

But with equal certainty I knew that if I did so my life would become an eternity of anticlimax. The choice lay between going into my house, and so coming face to face at last with the real R. A. Adcock, and turning away to become but a puppet figure on a Carousel, revolving endlessly at the behest of a mindless civilization.

It takes a long time to explain. It took much less to make the decision. I turned the hall light on and proceeded into my living-room-cum-study. The room itself is made from two, having had an intervening wall knocked down. A large window overlooks playing-fields, letting in light over my desk. Someone was sitting in my chair at my desk.

'I understand now why the driver made mistakes on the way back, so you'd have time to get here first,' I said, walking down the room towards the window.

My hands were cold and clammy. The creature looked up, and as I approached slowly turned its head. I caught my breath sharply as I recognized the shape of the creature. Myself.

'Perhaps you also understand why you were marked down from the first,' said my image in a clear but cold voice.

It was as if I were looking at a death mask of myself. I cannot begin to describe the uncanny quality of it.

'So you have decided I was right?' I asked.

'You are too good an advocate for your own good.'

'I suggest you quit, pack it in.'

'That is impossible,' said the voice harshly.

'You're committed to the Earth?'

'As committed as you are.'

'What are you going to do?'

'Take a little time to reconsider my position.'

'You might lose the second round as well as the first,' I said with more confidence than I felt.

'Eventually I shall win.'

'Perhaps,' I said with the fear welling up inside me once again. I took a last look at the creature sitting there at my desk and hurried outside into my garden.

I looked around in the bright sunshine, at the red brick of the house, the green of the grass, the flowers and the blue sky. As if my heart had missed a beat, blackness hit me for a brief moment. Then the light was there again. But instead of being in the garden I was in my room looking out through the window. Outside I saw a figure gazing up at the sky. Suddenly on the still air there came a gust of wind. I knew it from the bending of the long grass at the edge of the distant playing-fields, and from a cloud of dust that rose out of the dry earth. I looked again into the garden and saw it was empty. I looked everywhere around the room but I was the only person there.

The unfinished manuscript lay on my desk, the pages disturbed, as if by a reader. Rapidly I wrote the concluding section of this last chapter. As I reached the end of the penultimate sentence my last thought as a human was to add a large full stop. My first thought as a Molecule Man was one of stark horror, at the fantastically perverse creature with which I now had to deal.

THE MONSTER OF LOCH NESS

CHAPTER ONE

A FREAK STORM

The Highlands of Scotland are split by a trench, the Great Glen, stretching one hundred and fifty miles from Oban in the south to Inverness in the north. The two parts belong to different bits of the earth's crust, which move slowly against each other. Because of the grinding process and the glaciers of ten thousand years ago, the trench has been scoured deep, deep below sea level in some places.

From Oban an area of sea runs north for some fifty miles to Fort William. Here the land rises for ten miles before falling farther north to the bed of Loch Lochy. From Invergarry to Fort Augustus the land rises once more only to plunge into the abyss of Loch Ness which extends almost to Inverness.

Tom Cochrane was fast asleep, around midnight, when the storm broke. So intense was the rain that a torrent of water eventually found its way through the sturdy mountaineering tent. Sleep waned fast and suddenly Tom was wide awake, hearing the rushing water, feeling the wet soggy sleeping-bag, but seeing nothing. He cursed roundly the fact that he'd left his Land-Rover near Prince Charlie's cave, to the west of Loch Lochy and slightly east of Loch Arkaig. From that starting point he'd set out up Glen Cia-aig following a rough track for some five miles. The next morning he intended to climb Sron à Choire Ghairbh and Meall an Teangah for the simple reason that he'd never climbed them before. Then instead of returning to camp he would drop down to the western shore of Loch Lochy, make his way to Invergarry to stay with friends, and return to his camp the following day.

Tom's teeth chattered from time to time as he leant on an elbow listening to the rain. Not gentle drops, but the lashing of some cyclone let loose on this little valley just west of the Great Glen.

Tom Cochrane looked at himself in the mirror of reflective darkness. A one time reader in the department of geography at Edinburgh University, he had retired from this post at the early age of fifty-five. The university pension settlement wasn't much but it was at least something. More important to his financial position were three successful textbooks. Two were widely used in schools, the third, *Land Forms and Weather*, was now a standard university text throughout Britain and the Commonwealth, with some popularity in the U.S. as well.

Tom's capacity for liking people as people, not people in the abstract, was enormous. He would happily have gone on teaching if the whole trend in university education hadn't been towards a human battery farm producing disgruntled, egotistical chickens. Row upon row of long-haired bedraggled students wearied him, not for their appearance but for their lack of individuality, for which modern society was responsible. If only one of these same students had declared himself as an individual it would have been different.

Then there was Tom's wife, Flora. Temperamentally Flora was just the other way round. She liked people more in the abstract than individually. A busy, energetic woman, she had risen first to a professorship in the department of sociology, then to the august position of Dean of Women at Edinburgh. It didn't worry him unduly that Flora ranked higher in the university hierarchy than he did. But it did disturb him that Flora enjoyed incessant committee meetings, continual arranging of this or that, and endless entertaining of academic personnel in whom Tom hadn't the smallest interest.

So at the age of fifty-five, four years ago, Tom had beat a retreat from Edinburgh to the Highlands. He and Flora didn't 'separate' in the legal sense. In fact the new arrangement suited them both very well. There were times when Flora felt she needed a breather in the hills, and then Tom was always available. And Tom, whenever he felt a trace of boredom coming on, would return to the old life in Edinburgh. Usually a few days of this would send him scurrying back to the hills, where he and his ageing Land-Rover were now welcomed in every bothy and hamlet throughout the length and breadth of the Highlands.

He kept himself mentally alert by writing on days of bad weather, of which there were plenty. He'd managed another successful book, for summer tourists, telling them how the magnificent scenery had been sculptured in ancient times by vast flowing rivers of ice. Since, with few exceptions, he knew every hillside, its contours, flora and fauna, and since he was writing as a lifelong professional, the book was a guaranteed success.

Repeated attempts at fiction were much less remunerative, although occasionally he managed to get a short story published. This modest success pleased him mightily—for success in the things we can't do always seems more important than our real métier—but it made him realize too how the great short story teller is rarely the great novelist. We look to Tolstoy for novels not plays, to Chekhov for plays not novels. Shaw commands compulsive attention with the first speech from the stage, but even Patience herself would be bored stiff by his novels and prefaces.

There was another reason why Tom almost never found himself with spare time on his hands. Many years before, during his early university days, he'd been asked to teach a course involving a little statistics. Instead of learning the relevant mathematical processes by rote, as most non-mathematicians do, he'd made a sustained effort to find out what was really going on. From this beginning he had become fascinated by mathematics. Nowadays he always carried a mathemathical text with him. However he lacked the talent of the real mathematician, and even with that innate qualification he would still have been too late in the subject to have had any real chance of scaling the heights of mathematical understanding. But a bright intelligence combined with many years of study at least permitted him to gaze up at the peaks afar off. He knew their shapes, even if he could never actually reach them. And he knew quite enough by now of practical mathematics to give him a basis of genuine perception in the field of dynamical meteorology. This led him to an abiding absorption in clouds and air

movement from which extended a keen interest
birds and their migratory habits.

Tom's mind snapped back to reality as the s
of rain started to ease and the light strengthened
rummaged round, found his woolly cap and jammed it
on his greying hair. Once out of his bag he pulled a
pair of clean socks from his rucksack and started
to dress. The breeches were wet through as were
his shirt and old cashmere sweater. The dry socks
kept his feet warm until the water in the cold
leather of the climbing boots started to penetrate the
wool.

Swinging his rucksack over his shoulder he fastened
the entrance to the tent, and then after a last look round
took off uphill. The blood in his veins pounded until
he reached the top of Meall an Teangah. By this time
the misery of the night hours was forgotten, except
for a slight dampness.

The June morning had dawned clear blue and warm.
Because of a slight breeze he didn't remain long at the
summit cairn but cut rapidly down a pleasantly
shelving slope for six or seven hundred feet to a bealach
separating the two mountains. Here he spotted what
he thought were a pair of Canadian Snow Geese. This
strange sight puzzled him as he made his way up
Sron à Choire Ghairbh. Then on reaching the top he
again dropped swiftly down a ridge which plunged
steeply to Loch Lochy.

The bottom part was heavily wooded and it took a
little time to locate a fine ride running directly down
amongst the tightly packed trees to the lochside.
Tom took the ride almost at a run, making small

leaping diversions to avoid the tussocks and odd rotting trunks. Suddenly the ground came up at him as it levelled out. It was then that he saw a man lying face up just a few yards to his right. Tom stopped his forward momentum by sticking his boots hard into a tussock which gave under the strain. Then, struggling a few feet back the way he'd come, Tom stared down at the rigid corpse.

'Bloody birds,' he said as he looked at the empty eye sockets.

As he stood there a sound from the loch made him turn. For a moment he thought he was hearing things as the adrenalin pumped through his veins, but then he saw it—a boat moving slowly along the loch some half-mile from the shore. Tom removed his rucksack and covered the few remaining hundreds of feet to the lochside at extreme speed.

'Ahoy,' he yelled, hands cupped round his mouth to emphasize his baritone voice.

'Ahoy,' he called again, this time with a greater volume of air in his lungs.

The man in the boat appeared to turn, so Tom jumped up and down waving his arms frantically. His arms ached when at length the boat swung its bow towards the shore.

'What the hell's the matter?' called a tall blond young man as he threw the boat's anchor overboard some thirty yards away.

Tom raised a still aching arm and beckoned the fellow ashore. There was another infernal wait as a small rubber dinghy was launched over the side.

'You took your time,' was Tom's comment as he helped the blond-haired viking from the dinghy.

'Well, what's wrong?'

'Not big enough,' said Tom.

'What's not big enough?' scowled the young man.

'The dinghy.'

'How d'yeah mean?'

'Better come and take a look, young fellow, there's some trouble up ahead,' said Tom turning abruptly and starting off across the forestry road into the ride.

After a hundred feet or so Tom held his breath for a moment. Sure enough he could hear the heavy gasps coming from the young man behind him.

'Jesus,' was the breathy comment as the young man caught up with Tom on the little plateau where the dead man lay.

'The birds,' said Tom, as he looked at the now pale face of the young man. 'We'll have a bit of a job getting him down.'

'Man, you're crazy. What happened up here?'

'How should I know. Come on, I reckon we can manage to get him to your boat.'

'He can stay here for the police.'

'That's what I call public spirited,' muttered Tom. 'Leave the poor sod here, it's not my problem.'

'Then why do you want to bring him down?'

Tom thought for a moment. It had been his first instinct as a mountaineer. 'Maybe you're right. Come on, give me a hand to turn him over.'

The young man came trudging back and the two of them slowly turned the corpse over. It wasn't pleasant or easy as the ground was soft and uneven. Inevitably, the man's jacket pulled to one side and the shirt in the small of the back became exposed. It was stained brown. Tom lifted the fabric. There down the spine was a broad raw scar. 'Lightning,' he grunted. 'Last night's storm. When it hits a man, it goes right the way down the spinal column.'

'Nasty,' said the young man, his expression showing his relief that Tom hadn't had a part in the business. 'You recognize him?'

Tom shook his head. 'No, probably one of the foresters.'

Tom walked round familiarizing himself with the lie of the land.

'All right my boy, we'll be going. Maybe you'll give me a lift in that boat of yours, as far as Laggan. I can phone Fort Augustus from there.' Tom humped his rucksack up onto his back.

The young man was again left struggling with the descent in his sneakers.

'We can't get both of us in the dinghy,' he panted when he reached Tom.

'I can see that. Best bring the boat in closer. You can easily get within fifteen yards.'

'Going to swim for it?'

'Not bloody likely, come on let's get going.'

While the young man brought the boat inshore Tom cursed the fact that his pilot was a foreigner rather than a local, as in all conscience he didn't like leaving even a dead man out on the hillside.

When the boat was close to the shore, Tom heaved his climbing rope across the water. The young man attached it to the dinghy and within a few minutes

Tom was alongside. Then he saw the insignia of the boat. LOCH NESS RESEARCHES.

'So you're a monster man are you? Well now, who would have thought it. I can swap a few yarns on that subject,' Tom boomed in mirth as he climbed aboard.

The blond man remained silent as he pulled the dinghy on board.

'Researches, is it?' bellowed Tom.

'You said you wanted a lift.'

'Putting it politely. Commandeering your boat, if you like.'

This sudden shift to bellicosity was characteristic of Tom. If you were annoyed with him, he was annoyed with you, in double dose.

The two of them sat in silence as the boat moved to the north-east at about five knots. Tom looked critically at various pieces of equipment in the bow. He stood up and started examining a max-min thermometer, sample bottles and winch.

'Look, commandeering the boat doesn't give you the say-so to interfere with my equipment,' came the hard words from the young man at the tiller.

Tom picked up one of the sample bottles and moved to the stern of the boat.

'No it doesn't,' he yelled into the blond lad's face, 'Not at all, it doesn't. But why would a monster man be taking water samples? And in Lochy, not in Ness. That's what I'm wondering.'

'What's it to you?'

'My trade, at least it used to be, when I was at the University—Edinburgh. Look, I reckon we'd better introduce ourselves. Tom Cochrane.'

'John Stewart.'

Tom shook the youngster's free hand.

'But not from these parts. Western United States—eh?'

'That's right. How did you guess?'

'Got an ear for accents. Getting back to this,' Tom indicated the equipment, 'I did a survey myself of these lochs, a long time ago it was. Depths mostly, to reconstruct the old ice rivers, but some temperature work too.'

'Did you write it up?'

'Of course, but I don't carry it in my rucksack.'

'I'd like to see it.'

'Then you'll have to make a wee trip to Edinburgh.'

'I might just do that.'

'And you still wouldn't have answered my question. What the devil have water temperatures to do with monsters now?'

'Nothing, I guess.'

'Nothing, nothing! What the hell goes on?' roared Tom. John Stewart sighed, 'Look if you must know, jobs—real jobs—in my field—nuclear physics—aren't easy just at the moment, back in the U.S.'

'Ah-ha,' nodded Tom, 'so you're filling in over the summer. Pottering about, making measurements, instead of looking for monsters—eh?'

'Better than looking for Nessy.'

'Scepticism about Nessy, very good,' boomed Tom. 'Put me ashore just before you get into the Laggan locks.'

'O.K.'

The sweet scent of broom was suddenly strong as

they neared land. Stewart found a convenient spot, and was just on the point of flicking out the dinghy when he asked, 'What temperature would you expect—in the deepest part of Loch Ness I mean?'

'A bit above 4 degrees—centigrade. Maybe 5 degrees in places.'

'That's what I'd have thought.'

'That's what it is.' Tom took hold of the dinghy himself and skimmed it neatly out onto the water.

'No it isn't. It's a little above 7 degrees.'

Tom frowned and shook his head vigorously, 'Can't be. The bottom is fed by cold water, in winter—from melting snow. Sinks to the bottom after mixing a bit with the warmer water.'

'I know, but even so the temperature is over 7 degrees.'

'Not possible, young fellow.'

'I know it's not possible, unless there are strong turbidity currents.'

'Turbidity currents?' Tom paused to peer curiously up into the young man's face. 'I'll tell you what it is! It's a monster churning up the whole bloody lake!'

'I've wondered about that too,' murmured Stewart.

'You'd like it—I'll bet, a monster with three humps and a big flat head—fat-head more likely.'

'Which is where you're wrong, Mr Cochrane. I wouldn't like it at all, because it's crazy. But there has to be some explanation for the temperature.'

'I'll believe that when I see it.'

'You can measure it for yourself, any time you want to.'

'Not today, there's the poor fellow up on the hillside to look to. Tomorrow.'

'Tomorrow it is,' agreed Stewart brusquely.

'I'll be staying at Invergarry. There'll be a ceilidh o' the night,' shouted Tom as he paddled ashore. Once there, Stewart pulled the dinghy back and threw Tom his climbing rope. As the boat chugged in towards the lock Tom stood coiling his rope and pondering on the turbidity currents.

'Ridiculous, can't be as high as 7 degrees,' he stated with determination and set off to find a telephone.

CHAPTER TWO

THE CEILIDH

The ceilidh at Invergarry had resisted the usual modern dependence on the ever popular discotheque for its 'music'.

During daytime hours, Rory McDonald put petrol into cars. It was a humdrum job, but on the night of a ceilidh Rory was no ordinary mortal. He was one of three violins who made song, dance and joy into immediate reality. It never occurred to him that his garage job was humdrum, for most of the time he was whistling a tune or stamping out some ryhthmic pattern, to make sure he had it right.

Vast sums are currently being spent on research into industrial relations, on the odd notion that such issues are deep and subtle, requiring much careful investigation and dissection. In fact such issues are plain and elementary. They are utterly without solution, unless a meaning can be found to life, the same inner meaning which Rory McDonald found in his violin. All else, wages and salaries, are nonsense, or vanity, or insanity.

Ian Chisholm was different only in the respect that he was a shepherd, not a garage hand. But Angus Forrester was indeed something different, a one-time first violinist in the Glasgow Symphony Orchestra, forced into early retirement by delicate health. That was seven years ago, a good deal longer span than his doctor had 'given him' at the time. Angus never ceased to marvel at the fact that neither Rory nor Ian regarded the violin as a difficult instrument. Wrong notes never worried them—only breaking rhythm. To Rory and Ian the pipes were something else, requiring more than mortal skill. Usually the ceilidh at Invergarry lacked a piper but not on this particular night because Tom Cochrane was there. His friend Major Alistair Cameron of Drumnadrochit had been told of Tom's visit and had made the trip especially to give Tom a hard time of it with the sword dance.

Tom noticed John Stewart standing near the entrance to the hall. He watched the young fellow's movements for a moment and then strode towards him.

'You look as if you were needing a fine strapping lass to escort you through the dances.' Tom's voice boomed above the music.

'She hasn't arrived yet.'

'A woman's privilege to be late. Did you quarrel then?'

'No, just that Jeannie was driving through that freak storm last night.'

'Late to be on the road. She should have waited until it was over.'

'Exactly the argument.'

'So what's worrying you, the fact that she's regretting the unique moment of exhilaration with you or that she smacked herself into a ditch?'

'To be honest, probably both.'

'Aye well, if the young lady's Jeannie Macpherson

then you'll be glad to hear she's whole and hearty but the car had to be pulled from the ditch this morning. Rory McDonald told me she drives too fast.'

Tom gripped the lad's shoulder and then turned to join in the songs and dances which poured forth from the musicians at the far end of the hall.

From time to time during the evening Tom studied the people around him. The pretty young woman he saw showing John Stewart the paces he assumed to be Jeannie Macpherson. For a moment sadness cut through him as he realized the young couple would have been more at home on the crowded dance floor of some dim smoky discotheque than they were here in the land of their forefathers.

A hideous wailing sound outside the hall proclaimed the arrival of Alistair Cameron. The crowd scattered from the floor, each person taking a strategic position against some solid object. It reminded John Stewart of a wild-west bar with a gun fight imminent. Two crossed swords were placed in the middle of the floor, and Tom took up his stance close by, waiting for his tormentor to appear. The warming up process lasted a prodigious time, but in such awesome respect are the 'pipes' held throughout the Highlands that everybody listened in silent anticipation. The preliminaries over, Alistair had a tune well and truly going when he made his entrance. He was a short thickset man not unlike Tom in build.

The dance began, with Tom stepping sprightly amongst the blades. The dance itself started at a moderate tempo, then increased in speed from variation to variation.

There they were, two stocky men, one springing like a deer with furious concentration, as if his life depended on it, the other blowing fit to burst, eyes bulging, face crimson. Not a movement came from the onlookers as they seemed convinced that something had to give. Yet, miraculously the two somehow managed to bring the dance to a triumphant conclusion. Amid wild applause large tots of whisky were pressed upon them, which were downed at a single gulp.

'Aye, it would have been a fine dance, if young Alistair there had been in breath,' gasped Tom.

Before Alistair could retort and clear his reputation, the main door burst open, revealing a couple drenched by rain that now plummeted to earth outside but that none inside had even heard. Normally the couple would have passed unnoticed, a grey-haired, ample woman in spectacles and her slight, sandy-haired husband.

'We've seen it!' declared the woman.

The husband nodded.

'The monster!' the woman announced in triumph.

A grey-haired man in his early fifties moved from the floor towards the couple. Tom himself stepped over to listen.

'David Robinson, Department of Animal Ecology, Exeter. I'm in charge of "sightings" for LOCH NESS RESEARCHES.'

The woman recoiled a little from the gravity of this information.

'Sawyer, Ernest Sawyer,' said the husband.

'Tell us what you saw, Mr Sawyer.'

'We stopped to repair a puncture,' said Mrs

Sawyer, 'and this thing came up in the Loch and we ran down to the water's edge to see what it was. When it moved towards us, we knew then that it was alive.'

'How far away was it when it first came up?' inquired Robinson.

The couple looked for a moment at each other.

'I'd say about fifty yards,' answered Sawyer.

'In the dark too,' murmured Tom just loud enough for people close by to hear.

'And what did it look like?' asked Robinson.

'Well, it had three humps, and . . .'

This was as far as the man got before Tom burst in with a roar, 'I know, three humps and a long flat head.' Sawyer blinked for a moment at Tom.

'That's right,' he nodded, 'a long flat head.'

'I've got a long flat head,' bellowed Tom. 'I've got three humps and a long flat head.'

Tom began a grotesque dance, attempting to roll in the air like a porpoise. Rory McDonald and Ian Chisholm caught the spirit of the dance and scratched out an accompaniment to the wild cavortings. Everyone laughed, except Robinson and the Sawyers. Robinson's pale complexion was blotched with red as his anger grew. It was Mrs Sawyer however who made the challenge, when Tom had finished.

'We saw it, I tell you. We saw it,' she shouted passionately.

Tom saw the tears in the woman's eyes. He turned to Rory with a silent command and then grabbed hold of Mrs Sawyer as the violins started an old-fashioned Scottish waltz. Tom twirled the woman round the floor as if dancing with a peggy stick. At the end, to everyone's amazement, the woman stood there breathless and smiling.

'We'll have the newspapers in on this event,' Tom assured her, and even Mr Sawyer started to smile. Tom let Robinson lead the couple away for further interrogation while he himself sought out John and Jeannie. On reaching them he stared for a moment at the pretty young woman wishing he were somewhat younger.

In fact the girl was so bonny she almost made him forget the problem that had been puzzling him all afternoon and most of the evening. Why should lightning strike a man in a ride, especially when he was surrounded by tall trees? Surely the lightning would have struck a tree first?

CHAPTER THREE

THE KELPIE

The faint light strengthened slowly as Tom stumbled about in the kitchen of Rory McDonald's cottage. The taste of whisky was still strong in his mouth. In spite of the general disarray he managed to brew a pot of coffee and then sat quietly brooding, his usually clear bright mind darkened by the lightning, the freak storms and the temperature business. The figure that stuck in his mind was 5 degrees centigrade—not 7.

Into his train of disjointed thoughts squeaked the brakes of a Land-Rover. Stuffing himself into his anorak, retrieving the well-used rucksack, he gently unlocked the outer door, not wanting to disturb Rory's sleep.

'Good morning,' he said quietly as he slipped onto the front seat. Two sleepy faces greeted him.

They rattled in silence at some speed the ten miles from Invergarry to Invermoriston. Loch Ness, when they reached it, looked dark and distinctly sinister in the early morning light. Tom knew it would brighten and sparkle later on, as the morning heralded a beautiful day, but as it was now Tom had no fancy for it. He decided that Loch Ness in the half light was just the right sort of place for any self-respecting monster. No wonder most sightings were in the half-light.

Parking by the little jetty at Invermoriston, Tom said,

'I'll leave the rucksack here.'

'O.K. We'll start by filling up with gas,' replied John Stewart. Tom took out his camera, checking there was film, and placed it around his neck inside the anorak.

They carried jerry cans from the back of the Land-Rover to the boat and chugged out into the loch. Apart from Tom's attempt to keep cheerful, there was an air of disquiet. John headed the boat north towards the deepest part between Foyers and Urquhart Bay. All the while the sun climbed in a cloudless sky. The loch itself was still and smooth, reflecting at its edges the surrounding trees and cliffs.

Once in position the preparation of the equipment was simple. A max-min thermometer attached to a 20lb lead sinker on the end of a 1,000 feet of line. They lowered it on the winch, noting the foot markings on the line to give them the length they'd run out. At 650 feet they stopped, the line still taut, for at this depth the thermometer could not be much above the bottom of the loch. Jeannie produced cups of hot coffee from a flask, which they drank as they waited for the thermometer to adjust to its surroundings.

It needed only a few moments to haul the equipment and its sinker back on board, and to discover that the minimum temperature was indeed close to 7·5°C.

'Told you so,' murmured Stewart.

Tom stared at the thermometer, took off his woolly cap and scratched his head. What the hell could be wrong, he wondered. Maybe the line hadn't been vertical because the boat had been drifting, so maybe the equipment hadn't gone as deep as they thought. Or maybe there were underwater currents which had slanted the line. In the final analysis none of this seemed likely, considering the 20lb lead weight of the sinker.

'We'd better try again. Only this time we'll go right down to the bottom,' he said at length.

They hit the loch bed just after the markers on the line indicated that seven hundred and fifty feet had been payed out. Tom knew the loch to be about seven hundred feet deep, so it was clear the line couldn't have been far from vertical after all. John half expected the thermometer to be damaged but it wasn't, and this time it read $7 \cdot 8°C$.

'Higher than before,' said Jeannie.

To Tom there could be only one explanation, the thermometer was haywire.

'We'd better have it calibrated.'

'Not a bad idea. But we've got half a dozen of these things and they all give the same reading.'

'Maybe you've got a faulty batch.'

'Maybe. But Loch Lochy was near $5°C$, right where it should have been.'

'So that's what you were doing yesterday. Checking against Lochy.'

'Right. I don't have any calibration equipment, but I did have the other Lochs as a control.'

'Even so, we'd best do a lab check.'

'O.K.'

The two men stood for a while, deep in thought, gazing at the winch, the line, sinker and thermometer.

Could it be that something really was stirring up the whole loch? Tom dismissed the idea as ridiculous, just because there was such an enormous quantity of water. The damn loch was twenty-five miles long and one to two miles wide, say forty square miles of surface going down to an average depth of five hundred feet. Nothing in reason could mix that amount of water.

These thoughts were instantly shattered by a scream from Jeannie. Both men turned and looked in the direction she was pointing. A 'V'-shaped wake was approaching them about half a mile away. Jeannie took hold of John's arm as the three of them watched. Suddenly the wake subsided.

'The Kelpie,' Jeannie murmured, her voice trembling.

Out of the water rose a dark grey and black log, at least the first impression was that of a log.

If the Monster of Loch Ness had been shy hitherto in showing itself, it showed no shyness now. At its nearest point, Tom thought about one hundred and fifty yards, a snake-like head lifted six feet from the water. The neck must have been fully two feet thick. Behind was a great hump, like a monstrous camel. It seemed the appalling creature was as curious about them as they about it. Tom recovered quickly from the first shock, unzipped his anorak, quickly adjusted the light reading and started shooting with his camera. The monster, apparently gazing at them, swam round the boat a couple of times. Through the view finder Tom tried to see how many humps the animal had, sometimes it was three, sometimes just one. That's right, he thought to himself, one hump.

'Bloody hell,' he suddenly roared.

'What's up?' asked John turning to see Tom fiddling with his camera.

'No more film, left it in my rucksack. Come on, let's get as close as we can,' he grunted, pushing the camera back inside his anorak.

Still staring at the monster, John took what seemed an infinity of time to start the engine. Impatiently they closed the distance to some fifty yards. They could see beady eyes now, gazing fixedly in their direction. Then it was gone, diving deep into the dark lower waters of the loch.

'It must have been the engines that frightened it,' said Tom, watching Jeannie as she sat on the engine cowling.

'I reckon so. Lucky you got those pictures. Nobody would have believed us.'

'Blast it,' Tom grunted. 'I'd have liked a really close look, right down its throat.' Then he turned to Jeannie, 'How about a swim?'

Jeannie's eyes widened and she took John's hand.

For a while they cruised around the spot where the creature had disappeared. The first moments of exhilaration were soon replaced by a cold half-sweat. They were appalled at the nameless thing which had appeared so close to them. As if to match the change of mood, the sky clouded over quite suddenly. The loch was now forbiddingly sombre so that all three were glad to call off further exploration and experiments. Indeed one of the sudden storms for which Loch Ness is notorious was clearly on its way. A fierce wind now whipped up the former glassy surface and rain began to fall.

Long before they could reach the Invermoriston jetty the full fury of the storm hit them. They crouched as best they could in the well of the boat, near the steering gear, while the wind lashed the stinging rain into their faces. Suddenly lightning, followed instantly by an overwhelming thunderclap, lit the water ahead. Tom gripped John's arm fiercely.

'Look man, look over there,' he yelled above the wind.

Peering through the driving rain to the right they watched in horror as a fireball floated and danced on the water's surface.

'What the hell is that?'

'Fireball, keep clear of it on the left.'

John threw the tiller hard over, making the boat roll and kick like a wild stallion. The fireball disintegrated, flaming out in all directions. The surface of the loch became red like a prairie fire. Tongues flicked out evilly towards the boat. In spite of the shrieking wind they all had the impression of a strange smell, not the acrid smell of burning. At the climax of the storm the boat was shaken violently and decisively in a curious rhythm, almost as if it were being shaken purposely by some giant unseen hand.

An hour and a half later three bedraggled people staggered ashore at Invermoriston jetty, fervently thankful to be safe.

'I'll be making a wee trip down to Edinburgh,' said Tom, holding the thermometer, 'and I'll get this checked.'

They climbed unsteadily into the Land-Rover.

'Drop me at the hotel,' said Tom after they'd driven a little way.

'I wouldn't mind making the trip myself,' John remarked. 'Suppose we pick you up—about what time?'

Tom looked at his watch and was astonished to find it was still only 9.30 a.m.

'Make it eleven o'clock.'

'O.K. You can leave the thermometer—we'll bring it.'

John and Jeannie left Tom at the hotel. He watched them depart and then humped his rucksack to a small barn not far from the hotel. Here he changed into dry clothes. A couple of swallows circled around outside the barn door. He pondered on how such small birds could find their way to the Mediterranean, even North Africa. He decided there were many things he didn't understand, the freak storms being one of them. He didn't understand it one little bit. Loch Ness was well known for making its own weather, but not for the extremes of violence he'd just witnessed.

He stuffed his wet clothes into the rucksack, checked he'd left nothing, and made his way to the hotel with the summer sun now beating hard upon his back.

CHAPTER FOUR

EDINBURGH

A white shooting-brake appeared promptly at eleven. Tom waited and watched for a moment, then recognized Jeannie as the driver.

'There's no point in advertising. Someone would have noticed the Land-Rover going AWOL,' said John opening the rear passenger door.

'I was thinking of asking you to go round by Loch Arkaig.'

'Why Loch Arkaig?'

'Oh, I have my camp set up there. Better leave it though, 'tisn't good for the tent to be packed away wet too often.'

Tom squeezed himself and his rucksack among the piles of equipment on the back seat.

'Why these?' he asked, pulling a sample bottle from its rack.

'Oh, I thought there might be a chance of getting the water analysed.'

The strange smell from out on the loch came back to Tom's nostrils. It wasn't a bad idea, analysing the water, although at this moment his guess would be ozone.

Jeannie drove them by Spean Bridge, Laggan, Dalwhinnie and down the A9 to Perth, and from there on through Kinross, over the Forth Bridge, into Edinburgh. Tom's eyes remained firmly closed throughout most of the drive. After the first few miles of watching the road, he decided that if his number were up then he'd prefer not to know it. The knuckles of John's right hand were white as he gripped the back of the seat. From time to time, he whistled 'Oh Boy' through his teeth. On these occasions Tom would brace his legs in anticipation of the graunching, tearing sound of crumpling metal.

Tom opened his eyes as the momentum of the car was at last thankfully reduced to a snail's pace. After a moment he realized they were now on the outskirts of Edinburgh. He directed them to his house, near St George's Square.

'Hello,' said Tom as he pushed the front door open and saw Flora just about to pick up her gloves and handbag from the hall table.

'Oh, it's you.'

'As large as life, and how are you keeping,' he said, dumping his rucksack, smoothing his pullover · and giving his wife a peck on the cheek.

John and Jeannie came in, and for a moment Flora seemed overcome by John's Viking-like appearance.

'Let me introduce Jeannie Macpherson—daughter of *Sir* Ian Macpherson,' said Tom emphasizing the title. 'And this is John Stewart.'

'Haven't I seen you before somewhere? Women's hockey?'

'Golf, Mrs Cochrane,' said Jeannie.

'Ah yes, golf of course. Well, what are you all doing here?'

'Business—business,' boomed Tom.

'How long is this—business—going to last?'

'Nothing to worry about. A couple of days at most.'

'I'm not worrying—except about having the house turned into a bear garden.'

'We have no sinister intentions, Mrs Cochrane,' said John.

'I should think not. Sinister intentions are for Flora's friends. Where are you off to, my dear?'

'Senate meeting,' Flora bit off all superfluous words.

'Senate meeting. Now there are sinister intentions for you.'

'Don't take any notice of him, Mrs Cochrane,' said Jeannie, realizing Flora Cochrane wasn't too far away from flashpoint.

'Remember,' said Flora to Tom, 'no experiments this time.'

With this she was gone. 'No experiments,' mimicked Tom, 'and how should a man occupy himself except with experiments?'

While John and Jeannie installed themselves on the top floor of the terraced house, Tom busied himself with his camera. It appeared to have survived the freak storm, so he was reasonably hopeful that the film he'd shot of the Kelpie wouldn't be damaged.

Tom had no doubt about the value of his film. He'd been able to take a series of pictures of the Kelpie as it swam around the boat. By comparing them it would be obvious that the thing was real, particularly as in most shots the edges of the loch—the trees and cliffs—would show up well on the prints. The one thing that bothered him was that he'd been using colour film.

Black and white negative he could have developed himself, but as it was he'd have to send the film away, which he didn't like at all. He thought for a moment about maybe asking a local firm to do the job, then decided against it. Tom was no innocent in the world of publication and publicity. He knew just how easily valuable pictures can disappear. No, he thought, the best thing would be to send his cassette through the usual commercial channels. He addressed the label attached to the small tin, then nipped out to post it.

Tom's way of life was such that he had long since learnt to go by the sun. So, leaving John and Jeannie to their own devices, he was away to bed soon after dinner, and hard asleep by the time Flora returned. It also meant that Tom was awake at first light, about 4 a.m. in Edinburgh on a June morning. This time it was Flora who was fast asleep. Tom tip-toed out of the bedroom, descended two floors, made himself breakfast, and then rummaged about for the keys to the university department of geography. He'd kept his old keys to the lab but he couldn't find the main gate key.

He took a cup of freshly brewed tea back upstairs.

'Morning, morning,' he boomed.

Flora struggled slowly to consciousness and eventually managed to grasp the cup which Tom held out to her.

'It's a great day,' Tom went on. 'Where would your keys be? I've a mind to go down to the department library.'

'Keys, keys. In my handbag, in the hall closet.'

Tom left the bedroom quickly but not quite fast enough to escape the yell from Flora.

'It's only a quarter to five!' she screamed.

Tom drove the shooting brake to the University. An odd lorry or caravan trundled through the almost empty streets. It took a few minutes to open the main gate, drive the estate car through, and to relock. Then Tom was letting himself into his old department. It was more than a year now since he'd been there but every detail of the layout was well remembered. First however he rummaged in the back of the car to find the thermometer. He examined it carefully for a certain scratch mark, which he knew had been made by its passage on the bottom of Loch Ness. Tom had noted the scratch just before they'd sighted the Kelpie. Of course he'd hardly doubted that John would bring the right instrument. Even so, he wanted to be dead sure. Satisfied that he had the right one, he went into the department laboratory.

It took a few minutes to find where the lab thermometers were kept. At length he had them and selected one. He then simply filled a large bowl with water from the tap, and put John's thermometer and a lab one into it. The next step was to take a few ice cubes and to throw them into the water, to bring its temperature below that of the room. After the cubes had melted he checked the thermometer readings. They both read 12·3 degrees, as near as made no difference. Next he emptied more ice cubes into the water until they no longer melted. He found both thermometers now read zero, again as near as made no difference.

There seemed no doubt about it. John's instrument

was accurate from zero to twelve degrees. It was no longer possible therefore to doubt that the temperature of the lower water of Loch Ness was anything but 7·8°C.

Tom let himself into the department library. A quick reference to one of his own books showed that all previous work on the bottom water of Loch Ness had never given temperatures higher than 42°F. Conversion brought this figure to 5·5°C, more than two degrees below the latest measurement. Something really was stirring the waters of the loch, or at least so it seemed.

It was still only seven-thirty by the time he returned home. He made himself a pot of coffee and with the remaining water another pot of tea.

'Good morning,' he boomed at Flora as if nothing had happened. 'Beautiful morning.'

Before Flora was fully awake he'd replaced the new cup of tea for the old half empty cup, and retreated.

The others appeared downstairs, first Jeannie, then Flora and finally John. Flora was surprisingly mild. Soon Tom knew why.

'I'm glad you're home for the inauguration,' she said.

'What inauguration?'

'The Chancellor, of course. Don't pretend you didn't know.'

Tom did remember of course. He'd read about it in the newspapers. The new Chancellor was to be none other than the Prime Minister.

'You'll be having a grand time, my dear. And so will I, in camp. I found a great spot, in a wee valley above Loch Arkaig.'

171

'You'll be nowhere of the sort. Remember, Tom Cochrane, even if you're not on the faculty any longer, this is still your University.'

'When is it?'

'The day after tomorrow.'

Tom groaned. Three days wasted.

'As if anyone would miss us,' he grunted.

'They would, make no mistake about it,' concluded Flora.

In a sense Flora was right. Tom made an impression at receptions and banquets: her forte was committee work; Tom did better on extroverted occasions.

Jeannie had already left for a round of golf by the time John appeared.

'My, it's late,' he admitted.

'The day is well advanced,' agreed Tom. 'Coming up ten-thirty in fact.'

'I'll just rustle up a little brunch if that's O.K. Then we can see about that thermometer.'

'I've done that already.'

'What!'

'While you were sleeping like a log, my boy. Nothing to it—only an hour's work.'

'The thermometer was O.K. then?'

'Yes.'

'Well it had to be. But what does it mean?'

'Turbidity currents I suppose, like you said.'

'I've got an idea how that assumption can be tested.'

Tom frowned. 'Well, how?' he asked.

'Oxygen isotope, but I'll need a mass spectrometer.'

'What have oxygen isotopes to do with it? I thought you wanted the water analysed?'

172

'Not a chemical analysis—nuclear. There are three forms of oxygen, O^{16}, O^{17}, O^{18}, but for practical purposes we can forget about O^{17} because there's very little of it. The point is that most molecules of water, H_2O, have O^{16}, but something like one molecule in five hundred has O^{18}.'

'So what?'

'The two kinds of water have slightly different masses, different weights, which means the two kinds evaporate at slightly different rates. Rain water has slightly different proportions of the two forms compared with say ocean water. Even rain water falling at different times in the year will have different proportions, between winter and summer.'

'Ah-ha.'

Tom looked closely at John. The boy was more animated than he'd seen him yet. On his own ground now, which made a difference.

'You see just where this puts us,' continued John. 'If turbidity currents are stirring Loch Ness, the water will be the same everywhere—surface and bottom water. But if the loch isn't mixed then the surface will be different from the bottom.'

'Because the bottom water comes in winter mostly, and the top in summer,' concluded Tom.

'Right.'

'And what's this mass-whatever-it-is instrument you need?'

'A mass spectrometer. It separates the O^{16} and O^{18}. There must be one in the University. Every modern lab has one.'

Tom got to his feet.

'I'll find out soon enough.'

He was away to the phone in the study on the first floor. Meanwhile John occupied himself with preliminary calculations.

'They have one,' said Tom on his return. 'We'll go down to the physics department right away and see what we can do about getting access to it.'

'How much should we tell them?'

'Not more than we need.'

'That I'm examining water circulation?'

'Something like that.'

'O.K. Just give me time to freshen up.'

While he waited, Tom pondered about turbidity currents. It didn't make sense. There couldn't be that amount of silt going into the loch. He wondered about the freak storms. That didn't make much sense either. In fact, he concluded, nothing made sense.

From the moment he and John went into the physics laboratory, Tom saw he'd better leave the lad to his own devices. He made a few introductions but clearly John knew his way around in such a place. After half an hour or so Tom decided he was out of place and he'd better fill in his time until the blasted inauguration by looking up a fistful of references in the university library.

Inexorably the time for the inauguration came round. Tom visited the barber for a haircut and put on a newly pressed suit, which made him feel uncomfortable. He drove Flora's smart prestige car to a specially reserved parking-lot. Flora spent the time during their drive lecturing him on the etiquette necessary for such an occasion. Instead of listening he kept contrasting his present situation with the wild ride he'd had in his old Land-Rover up the little valley above Loch Arkaig. The really remarkable thing was that two ways of life, Edinburgh and Loch Arkaig, should exist side by side with each other. Tom wondered if his life in the Highlands would be at all possible without the existence of Edinburgh. Regretfully he decided it wouldn't, for, without the cities, the Highlands would soon relapse into an unco-ordinated wilderness. He decided in all honesty that he was having the best of both worlds.

The inauguration was like all inaugurations, a formal ceremony followed by a reception. There was the usual crowd, making an occasion of the event. Tom had been right in saying that his absence would not have been noticed. It was his presence that was noticed. Flora had sensed, correctly, that this would be so—and in so far as Tom was noticed so was she. Rightly, for on such occasions it is proper that the pillars of the University should be plainly in evidence.

Tom was noticed as usual for his powerful baritone voice. However loud the din, Tom could easily ride above it. Inevitably, because he could be heard, he always gathered a crowd around him, listening to his anecdotes. Especially today for at one point he decided to mimic the flight of a marsh harrier which resembled that of a VTOL. Inevitably too, Tom found himself talking to the chief guest, the new Chancellor, the Prime Minister. This wasn't because Tom pushed himself forward. It was rather that other people for the most part were shy and backward, whereas Tom confronted the P.M. in just the same way he confronted everyone else.

The P.M. looked remarkably cheerful, which struck Tom as pleasant considering the enormous pressures the man had come under since taking office.

'Nothing I've read lately in the papers, Prime Minister, would seem to justify your present good humour,' Tom boomed.

'But surely this is an occasion for me to be in the best of spirits?' boomed the P.M. in reply.

'If you'll excuse my saying so, there's nothing here to justify anything but the most gloomy forebodings.'

'Gloomy forebodings?'

'Yes, Prime Minister. Look at them all, chattering and shouting and drinking. Apes, Prime Minister. It's a party of apes you've joined. By the way, there's a fellow behind you with a tray of drinks. Don't let him get away with them.'

The Prime Minister grabbed a couple of drinks, handed one to Tom and roared with laughter. This was the moment the press had been waiting for. There was a blinding flash of bulbs from the cameramen. On the morrow, millions would note the P.M. bellowing with laughter, with a raised glass, and would wonder what the hell was going on.

'Actually,' roared the P.M., 'I'm off on a holiday tomorrow. Ten days with the yacht,' he roared again.

'Where?' boomed Tom.

'Haven't decided exactly where. It's standing off Helensburgh at the moment.'

'You know the Highlands, sir?'

'Never been before, but always wanted to.'

'Better make for the Strait of Corryvreckan.'

'Not a bad idea.'

'How about joining the search for the Monster?' Tom added.

'Monster?'

'Loch Ness.'

'How does that business stand these days?'

'Very prosperous, I believe,' answered Tom.

By this time various dignitaries who had been waiting to talk to the P.M. felt they'd had enough nonsense, and bore down on the two of them. Tom immediately gave way, not because of any sense of impropriety, but because he'd just spotted Flora scowling at him. He crossed the floor to find out what the thundercloud look was all about.

Flora waited until they were on their way home before lecturing him. Who the devil did he think he was, pushing himself forward like that, she wanted to know. Tom had a general idea of what she meant but he didn't agree. If it came right down to it he thought they were all a bit daft, Flora included. Besides those turbidity currents and the freak storms were still worrying him.

John was waiting for them when they arrived back. From the look in the lad's eyes Tom knew he was onto something.

'Well, what's up?' Tom asked when Flora had thumped upstairs.

'I'm desperately in need of samples from some of the other lochs, the deep lochs. Jeannie is going back to try and get them. Will you help her?'

'What sort of samples?'

'Just surface and bottom water, the same as Loch Ness.'

'How did the oxygen isotope idea turn out?'

'It went O.K. I've found that the surface and bottom waters aren't the same. The water hasn't been mixed.'

'You mean the turbidity current idea . . .'

'Can't be right.'

'But the temperatures . . .'

'I've got a clue, and it's wild. But I need water from other lochs—as a control.'

'You'd better calm down a bit, young fellow, and explain what you're up to.'

'I don't want to talk in the middle of an experiment.'

'You want to go on working here in Edinburgh while Jeannie and I collect the samples. Is that it?'

'Right. I want you to collect them and Jeannie to get them back here.'

'More like soda water when they arrive I should think,' murmured Tom. 'Can't you give me some idea . . .'

'No, you'll have to wait I'm afraid.'

John was vastly more commanding now than before. Got the bit between his teeth, Tom thought.

'Well, I'll hardly be weeping, getting away from Edinburgh. Have you any preference as to lochs?'

'Not really, so long as they're deep. Except that I'd like Morar to be one of them.'

Tom stood in silence. Morar is it now, he thought to himself. He wondered whether they'd had any freak storms in or around Loch Morar recently.

CHAPTER FIVE

THE WATER SAMPLES

By the time he and Jeannie set out the following morning Tom had put in a fair amount of work. If there was one thing he knew backwards it was how to organize a field expedition. This was like the old days, and in truth he was enjoying it.

After checking the sample bottles, sinkers and lines, he found that a few useful things were missing so he went back to the geography department where he borrowed several odds and ends he needed. It was particularly important to equip himself with photocopies of maps of the lochs, maps which gave details of depths. Tom rejected John's suggestion of using a rubber dinghy. He'd no intention of being caught in a storm half a mile from shore in such a flimsy contraption. He knew highlandmen with boats, on Lochs Tay, Ericht, Arkaig, Quoich, Mullardoch and Morar, but had drawn a blank in the difficult case of Loch Treig.

Jeannie was amazed at the speed with which the expedition developed. They were away from Edinburgh by 6 a.m. the morning after the inauguration. By 8 a.m. they were rowing out on to Loch Tay, or rather Jamie Campbell—Tom's friend in those parts— was doing the rowing. The samples were soon gathered, Tom taking extreme care in the labelling and entries in his notebook, for future cross-checking. After a short stop for coffee at Kenmore, they were soon at Dalwhinnie where the same process was carried out on Loch Ericht, except that here they used a motor-boat to reach the deepest part of the loch some six miles from the jetty.

The expedition continued through Laggan, Spean Bridge, along the western end of Loch Lochy, through Gairlochy to the hill track that led to Tom's camp.

'You certainly choose inaccessible places,' remarked Jeannie after she'd finished the last hair-raising mile of bouldered track.

'Inaccessible to humans but not to nature.'

'Are you sure you don't want me to come with you?' asked Jeannie.

'No, no. I can manage fine now. You'd best be on your way to Edinburgh. That young man of yours will be champing on the bit by now.'

'You've got the arrangements clear?' asked Jeannie, colouring a little at Tom's innocent statement.

'Yes, certainly. When I've got all the samples safe and sound I'm to meet you at your parents' home in Errogie. Let's see, three days from now.'

Jeannie nodded and smiled, revved the engine and was about to depart.

'Hey,' yelled Tom, 'not quite so fast. I want that equipment out before you go.'

With a wry smile Jeannie helped him remove the equipment. When she had gone Tom shook his head. Young people, he thought, all speed and confusion, without method.

Tom cursed the sticky door lock on his Land-

Rover, finally giving the whole attachment a kick. This time the key turned the barrel and the door creaked open. He carefully packed the equipment out of sight behind the spare wheel, relocked the door and set out on foot up the valley to where he'd left the rest of his gear. By the time he reached the tent a slight dew was beginning to settle. He disregarded his first idea of breaking camp and returning to the Land-Rover for the night, deciding to spend the night where he was. A quick look round revealed that little was amiss, so he prepared for bed.

The following morning Tom was up with the light, as usual. He made a pot of tea and sat contemplating for a while as the dew on the tent evaporated. At length he had everything packed in its respective bag, and was soon marching back to the Land-Rover, looking a little like a sherpa with his bulky rucksack.

The Land-Rover refused to start. Tom sat there a moment before releasing the hand brake to allow the vehicle to roll forwards. He waited for speed to build up and then released the clutch. The vehicle bucked to a halt. 'Sod,' exclaimed Tom to himself. The freewheeling and bucking to a halt continued for a further half-mile before Tom pulled the handbrake on and got out. With the bonnet up he inspected the ignition leads. They all seemed secure. Then a wry smile crossed his face. A quick search in the bottom of his rucksack produced the rotor arm which he quickly fitted. A little more free-wheeling and the engine purred into life. The rough hillside track soon made way for the metalled road. With a roar from the engine Tom was now on his way.

Collecting all the samples took longer than Tom had expected, four days instead of two, or possibly three. Arkaig, Morar and Quoich went reasonably well, for the weather was fine and settled. Loch Mullardoch proved different.

Tom spent the night of the second day in the cottage of Willie Ferguson, near Cozac Lodge in Glen Cannich, preferring to occupy the evening yarning with Willie instead of staying at the Lodge. This had been converted into a hotel after the ruination brought on the country-side by the Highlands Hydro-electric Board. These days no self-respecting laird would have anything to do with the place.

The following morning Tom and Willie humped the outboard motor to the edge of the loch, above the hydro-electric dam wall, where Willie had beached his dinghy. Tom observed his surroundings with disgust. The vivid beauty of the loch and of the river running through the glen had gone. Tom would happily have lynched the men of the Hydro Board, sitting in offices making paper plans for desecrating wild and beautiful scenery.

'Come on, man,' called Willie, struggling with the boat.

'Aye.'

They launched the boat, started the outboard and chugged gently four miles to the west of the dam. Everything went well so far as collecting the samples was concerned. Tom knew exactly where he wanted them from. But with the water safely gathered, he had the idea that he'd like to climb Beinn Fhionnliadh, a remote mountain near the western end of the loch.

This was one of the few he hadn't climbed, because of its extreme isolation. Willie was happy with the plan as there were cattle pasturing on the north shore he wanted to take a look at.

Willie dropped Tom near the loch head. They agreed to meet again in four hours. As the boat pulled out into the loch the engine died. Tom turned to see whether he should stay and help but Willie waved him off.

The day was brilliantly fine, with the sun blazing down from an almost cloudless sky. Tom started steeply uphill. Driving hard with his legs gave him satisfaction. Height came quickly, and soon he was looking back a thousand feet down to the sparkling water of the loch. He looked at the water for a while until he spotted Willie's boat moving steadily to the northern shore. Still the mountain rose ahead at an unrelenting angle, another two thousand feet. Tom enjoyed every step of it.

At the top he eased his pace and looked at his watch. An hour and fifty minutes up, an hour down, he thought, which would give him about an hour on top. He sat down by the summit cairn and browsed in the sunshine.

Tom woke instantly with the first puff of cold air. A day which had dawned gloriously fine had now turned into a day of trouble. Cold and warm air mixing spells foul weather. The water vapour in the warm air condenses. The energy of condensation drives the mixing process faster and faster, which brings forth wind and rain spiced by thunder and lightning. The chill of the wind told Tom that it was going to be bad. Without hesitation he dug into his rucksack, donned his waterpoof overgarments, and then started quickly off downhill.

The sky darkened with amazing rapidity. A third of the way down the rain started. Tom was worried, not about himself—he'd been wet before and another soaking wouldn't harm him—but Willie was out there on the loch in an open boat.

Most people think the weathering which occurs in the hills happens more or less continuously down the years, that each inch of rainfall has about the same effect as every other inch. But weathering occurs mainly in occasional storms of great intensity, such as the one that hit Tom. Lightning striking the hillsides plays the dominant role in exposing underlying rock. It rips down a hillside from top to bottom leaving a trail of stones and boulders in its wake, boulders in unstable positions which subsequently roll devastatingly downward as they are dislodged by torrents and by the frosts of winter.

Lightning played increasingly around by the time Tom reached the shore. In appalling contrast to its earlier placidity the water was now churning in a fierce wind. If Willie had a grain of sense, Tom thought, he would have put ashore as soon as he saw the signs of the storm, and would be making his way on foot back to Cozac. But what if Willie were still out there making his way to the rendezvous point? Tom found a makeshift shelter under a little cliff and settled down as best he could.

The storm raged on unabated throughout the afternoon. Lightning flashes and thunder were essentially synchronous. Then suddenly as if by magic the wind was gone. Half an hour later the rain stopped, leaving to Tom's amazement a blanket of mist which covered everything, in zero visibility. It was now much more like the prelude to than the end of the storm. Tom was shivering with cold, and the sinister blanket that surrounded him didn't make him feel any better. The thick mist meant that Willie would have very little chance of finding the pick-up point, assuming the man was insane enough to be still out there on the water. Tom waited in the stillness, listening, but there was no sound of an engine.

At first he was thankful to stride out with as much energy as he could muster, to get a little circulation through his chilled limbs. The desperately rough terrain however soon brought curses from Tom, unable to really see where his feet were going. He'd been sour enough in the morning sunshine about the hydro-electric inundation of the old pathways. Now he had to suffer in long, bitter earnest. Given the old pathway he would have reached Cozac Lodge in three hours. He'd be lucky now to be back there by midnight.

Three miles from the dam, just when he felt he was getting to grips with this abominable walk, he hit a worse horror. The old path would have taken him on the south side for a while, but would have crossed to the north on a spit of land near Benula Lodge. Now the spit was submerged, forcing him into what had once been pleasant woodland. But no longer. A foolhardy owner had cut the trees before discovering that it was uneconomical to transport them down the Cannich Valley. Consequently the fallen timber had been left to rot. Tom stumbled through a nightmare jungle until he was forced to stand and shriek curses at the world around him.

At the dam his tribulations didn't end. The gate across the dam was locked, and because it was part of a small control building it was impossible to climb over. He dropped down below the dam wall and crossed the river, now in violent spate. There was just the faintest light in the western sky as he managed to haul himself out onto the northern bank. Half an hour later he stumbled into Willie Ferguson's cottage.

Willie had seen sense all right, but on Tom's arrival at the cottage all he could do was apologize for not arriving at the rendezvous point. 'But ye'll understan', the sky was a black as the de'il's ass,' Willie muttered as he prepared a bowl of soup, mindful of the theological teachings of his presbyterian fathers.

The following day dawned brilliantly fine once again. When the weather had the settled appearance of long clear sunny days Tom found it hard to recall the previous day's storm. The two men set out along the north shore to retrieve the dinghy. A couple of miles west of the dam wall, near the site of the one-time habitation of Mullardoch, Willie suddenly stopped and gazed out over the loch.

'What is it, man?' asked Tom, for he was impatient to reach the dinghy. Willie stood there shaking his head. Then he resumed his slow measured stride, and muttered, 'I'm no' speaking.'

The Allt Taige burn was still in full spate. It wasn't easy to cross. Tom, not in any mood to trifle with it—after his river crossing the previous evening—

went right ahead instead of bothering to hunt around upstream for a more strategic point. He jumped precariously from rock to rock and was rewarded for his boldness by reaching the far bank without immersion. Willie wasn't so lucky. Tom helped him out with a good hefty pull, remarking 'and now are ye speaking,' as he did so. Willie grinned as he took off his boots and squeezed out his socks.

'Ye'll be thinking I'm daft.'

'I won't. I've been knowing you're daft for a long time,' answered Tom.

'Not as daft as this.'

'This what?'

'This thing out on the water.'

Willie methodically shook out his socks and began putting them on again. Tom sat on a rock waiting, knowing it was little good trying to force anything from Willie.

'Aye, it was a strange thing, a ball of fire, out there on the loch.'

'When?'

'When I was coming back, yesterday.'

'How about the mist?'

'It seemed to burn away the mist.'

'How big would you say it was?'

'I don't know. Fifty or hundred feet across, I couldn't be sure. A hundred feet more like.'

'On the water?'

'Aye, riding on the water it seemed.'

'Did it move?'

'I believe so, but the mist made it hard to see. It was full of the colours of the rainbow.'

'Colour?'

'Aye, colour. Colours of a rainbow.'

They came to a rough bit of ground and took different routes to cross it When they again came together they walked on in silence.

It was gratifying to find the little boat where Willie had left it. After bailing out most of the water they were able to turn the boat over and empty out the rest. The outboard presented a more tedious problem, since the electrical parts had to be dried. This took time, but obligingly, on the third pull of the starting rope the engine spluttered into life, and half an hour's steady progress brought them back to where the samples had been collected the previous day. Tom thought it advisable to start afresh even though the samples appeared intact after their adventure.

So Tom Cochrane was delayed by almost two days in his expected time of arrival at the home of Sir Ian Macpherson in Errogie. He swung the Land-Rover in front of the large stone house. A servant appeared shortly after Tom had pulled the bell rope.

'Mr Cochrane,' boomed Tom as he strode past the man into a vast hall. The retainer departed, as uncommunicative as when he opened the door.

From one corner of the hall a curving flight of stairs mounted aloft. Tom surveyed the walls with their tapestries, swords and shields. What he found unusual, on close inspection, was a vast rendering of the 'Macpherson cat' embossed in stone on one of the walls.

Sir Ian Macpherson was a big man, tall, with plenty of weight but without being fat. He was red of face with hair midway between sandy and auburn, in contrast to Jeannie who was a throwback to the 'dark' side of the Macpherson clan. Sir Ian strode about his estate with a long stick of considerable thickness which he grasped with a leather gauntlet. He wore the Macpherson tartan as everyday attire but not the bonnet, which he regarded as only proper on occasions of state or war.

'You must be Jeannie's friend, Tom Cochrane,' said Sir Ian towering over Tom.

'Aye. I have some things for her to take to Edinburgh.'

'She's away on the golf now.'

'She'll be doing that all right,' nodded Tom, relapsing into the non-committal manner of the gaelic highlander.

'You'll be taking a drop?'

'Aye, that would be most kind.'

Tom followed Sir Ian into a large room filled with the usual bric-à-brac which passes in the highlands for family treasures. Macpherson sloshed whisky into two tumblers and handed one to Tom.

'Slainté,' he proposed in a loud tenor.

'Slainté,' replied Tom in his lowest and gravest bass.

He downed precisely a half of the whisky, avoiding both the affected southern practice of sipping and the vulgar highland practice of gulping the lot. Both men stood there breathing hard as the fire worked its way from throat to belly.

'Ah, that's a fine drop,' remarked Tom in a reverent kind of way.

His host stood for a moment and then gave the

signal for the second half. Both men raised their glasses simultaneously. Then the whisky was gone and both were breathing hard once more.

'Daddy! Drinking before tea time!'

Jeannie was there, a bag of clubs over her shoulder, a picture of glowing health. In mild intoxication, Tom contrasted daughter and father and thought it a pity that humans weren't like whisky, improved with age.

'I've got something for you, Tom,' Jeannie announced.

She was gone from the room for a moment, returning with a small packet which Tom knew to be a box of transparencies. For the first time in years he was excited to the point where his heart seemed to be in his mouth. He ripped away the wrapping, took the box to a big octagonal wooden table and opened it. With unsteady hands he shook out the transparencies and held a couple of them up to the light. There indeed was the Kelpie, just as it should be, in focus—needle sharp. This was real proof, for the first time. No doubt about the Monster now. Tom completely overlooked his former scepticism. He was an enthusiast now. He handed a transparency to Jeannie and another to Sir Ian.

With a half-stifled shout, Sir Ian rushed over to a sideboard.

'What are you looking for, Daddy?'

'That viewing spyglass thing.'

Jeannie joined in the search.

'Have you a projector?' asked Tom.

Jeannie found the viewer, then shook her head at Tom's question.

Incredible, thought Tom, a viewer but no projector.

Sir Ian peered into the viewer and then shouted full-bloodedly, 'The Kelpie. It's the Kelpie!'

Grasping the viewer, Sir Ian raced twice around the room, like an enormous dog. Opening a door, he shouted again, 'Annie! Annie, come and look.' Moments later a quiet grave-faced woman entered the room. Tom always marvelled at the reserve of the ladies of these highland landlords, except there was one who had once given him a lot of jaw-jaw, over in the Ossian region.

'Now what is it?'

'Take a look.'

Lady Ann peered into the viewer.

'Why, it's the Kelpie,' she said calmly, as if the creature in the viewer were a normal feature of every-day life. 'So that's what you've been up to these days, with that American boy.'

'I wish those damned Americans would stop messing about with our monster,' complained Sir Ian loudly.

'I'll get you a print of it,' offered Tom.

With a muttered exclamation Sir Ian strode out to the entrance hall. Here he gazed at a wall covered in tapestry. 'We'll have a great picture of the Kelpie mounted there.'

Tom had no doubt that his transparency, sharp as it was, couldn't be blown up to six feet by eight.

'Wouldn't it be as well, embossed in stone, as the Cat is,' observed Tom.

'Ah-ha! There's an idea for you, Annie. I'll have Gideon Urquhart start on it in the morning.'

'I'm sure Gideon has other work he must finish

before he can start a new job for you, dear,' said Lady
Ann mildly.

'We'll see about that. What's his phone number?'

'You'll find it in my black book, dear.'

'Yes, but where's your black book?'

'By the telephone, dear.'

Then Sir Ian was gone, followed closely by his wife.

'It'll take at least a week to get prints,' said Tom.

'Don't worry,' Jeannie replied. 'He'll forget about it
as soon as he remembers his new forestry project. I'll
tell him there's a fire hazard, or something.'

'I've got the other samples. When are you taking
them down to Edinburgh?'

'After tea. John is shouting for them, so I'd better
get down there tonight.'

'Shouting? Has he found something?'

'He's terrifically excited.'

'About what?'

'I don't know. He won't say.'

Tom grunted.

The two of them went out to the Land-Rover and
transferred the sample bottles to the shooting brake.

'Those pictures—you know they're valuable,' said
Jeannie.

'I think they might be,' said Tom securing the last
bottle.

'Well, John asked me to have a word with you about
them.'

'Oh?'

'He doesn't want a share of them, if that's what
you're thinking,' said Jeannie with a sharp protective
look.

'I wasn't thinking . . .'

'Oh yes you were. I could see it on your face.'

'Well, for that matter, John would deserve a share wouldn't he? After all, I was out in his boat.'

'That's not the point. It's just that he doesn't want you to give them away. Like selling them to a newspaper for £50, or something like that.'

'Well, I hadn't decided . . .'

'Isn't that what you were going to do?'

'I might.'

'John says you should take them to Loch Ness Researches. You should ask a *lot* for them.'

'What does he mean by a lot?'

'He said more than you could possibly imagine.'

Tom's deep chuckle rang out, 'I can imagine a lot.'

'John said you couldn't.'

'We'll see. Where do I find the boss?'

'They have an office in Inverness.'

'Loch Ness Researches?'

'Yes, but John said to tell you that L.N.R. is really only the subsidiary company. So it's no good going to them. The real boss—I've got his address somewhere,' said Jeannie, recovering her handbag from the shooting-brake. At length she found a small sheet of notepaper and handed it to Tom.

'Thanks.'

Tom read the address: 16 Dingwall Terrace Gardens, Inverness.

By the time Jeannie had left for Edinburgh, and Tom had managed to extricate himself from another whisky drinking session with Sir Ian, it was too late to head for Inverness. Instead he went back to Invergarry and

Rory McDonald. He spent the evening yarning about storms, ghosts and little people, so that he had Rory in a nervous condition before they turned in.

It was nearly 10 a.m. by the time he reached Dingwall Terrace Gardens the following morning. He parked, collected the box of transparencies, and walked to Number 16. Above the door was a large notice, in stylish gold lettering announcing that the occupants were:

DR BALLDRAGON AND ASSOCIATES

CHAPTER SIX

LOCH NESS RESEARCHES

The interior of Number 16 was fitted out in a lavish style. This was reassuring, considering the nature of Tom's errand. Whoever was running this show obviously enjoyed his creature comforts, unlike the poor devils of employees in their leaky caravans along the shore of Loch Ness.

Tom knocked on the door marked inquiries and walked in. Seated at a desk, well set back from the door, was a woman whom Tom judged to be about thirty. She wore a grey wig which brought out her fresh, clear complexion. For a moment she reminded Tom distinctly of the eighteenth century, like the door he'd just come through. In fact she reminded him of Despina in Mozart's *Cosi Fan Tutte*.

'Can I help you?' she asked in a voice quite as deep as Tom's own.

'I'd like to see the boss,' he said in crude twentieth-century style.

'Dr Balldragon is occupied at the moment.'

'Do you come from these parts?'

'Oh no, I come from London.'

'You must find it quite a change.'

'Indeed.'

This was some secretary, thought Tom. More like

an elocution teacher, except it was plain she had no wish for conversation. He waited a few minutes, occupying himself in arranging his transparencies. There came a gentle tinkle, no distastefully harsh telephone bell here. Despina rose from her desk, floated across the room, opened a door, left Tom alone for a moment, and then returned.

'Dr Balldragon will see you now, Mr—?'

'Cochrane.'

Despina sailed ahead of him and announced 'Mr Cochrane,' and then withdrew, closing the door.

Dr Balldragon was seated at a very large desk, empty of papers. At a glance it was clear that Balldragon was naturally very strong. He was big-chested without seeming thick set, like Tom. The fact that he was completely bald seemed to reflect on Despina's wig somehow. He crushed the stump of a cigar, rose from his desk and came forward to meet Tom with outstretched hand. There was something about the manner of it that put Tom on his guard, which was fortunate, for the grip of the man's hand was ferocious.

'Have a cigar, Mr Cochrane,' he said, returning to his desk and producing two from a box.

'I don't, not at this time of day, only after dinner.'

'Well, what can I do for you, Mr Cochrane?'

'It would be easier to explain if you had a projector for 35-mm still pictures.'

'Oh, you've got a picture of the monster! I guessed as much. We have fifty people a week coming in here with pictures of the monster. All wanting to flog them at fifty pounds a time. Does it have three humps and a long flat head?'

'As a matter of fact it does.'

'Sometimes it's a floating log. Sometimes it's a mass of water-soaked vegetation. Sometimes it's a plain fake. Which of those is yours, Mr Cochrane? Or have you found some new gimmick?'

Tom forebore to inform Balldragon that from the moment he'd come into the room his projected sale price had been steadily rising.

'It would be easier to decide if you saw them for yourself, wouldn't it?' he suggested.

'It would be wasting my time, don't you think?'

Smoke rose lazily above the desk.

'You don't believe in the monster, Doctor?'

For answer Balldragon bellowed with laughter. This caused him to swallow smoke, so that in the end there was an inevitable explosion from the man. Despina came in carrying a glass of water.

'Are you all right, Doctor?' she asked anxiously.

'I'm fine, Susie, just fine,' he spluttered.

So the real name was Susie. Pity.

'Is the projector set up?' asked Balldragon.

'Ciné?'

'No, stills.'

'I could have it ready in five minutes.'

'Set it up.'

'Yes, Doctor.'

When Despina had withdrawn for the second time, Tom asked, 'If you don't believe in this Kelpie, why do you go on running this show?'

Again Balldragon laughed, this time avoiding the smoke.

'It isn't what I believe that matters, Mr Cochrane.

It's what other people believe. That's the first principle of business.'

'You take care to employ people who do believe—eh?'

'Naturally.'

'How about Dr Stewart?'

Balldragon frowned. Then he pulled a thin file from a capacious bottom drawer of the desk.

'Ah, yes. John James Stewart, Doctor of Philosophy, California Institute of Technology. Employed for his qualifications of course,' said Balldragon looking up from the file.

'Gives a *bona fide* scientific tinge to the whole enterprise?'

'Exactly.'

Susie—Despina—opened the door and announced that the projector was ready, her voice still entombed in the bass clef.

They went into a small room which seemed designed for the purpose. 'We have a lot of film of our own,' said Balldragon, as if he felt some explanation was required. Tom transferred some but not all of his pictures into the cassette of the automatic projector. With everything ready he switched on the lamp and slowly went through the slides, showing the Kelpie swimming just once around the boat.

Balldragon took Tom's place at the projector. He grimaced as he went through the sequence for himself. Tom could see the fellow's teeth were strong and perfect, reminding Tom uncomfortably of his next visit to the dentist. Oddly enough, Balldragon, the very man who should have had profound faith in the existence of the monster, was searching for some sign of a fake.

He ran through the sequence again, now very quickly, so you almost felt as if you could see the monster swimming around. At length he indicated that they should return to his office. Tom collected the slides and followed.

'Well,' said Balldragon on reaching his office.

'Five thousand,' answered Tom smartly.

'Five thousand?'

'Five thousand pounds.'

The immediate astonishment on the man's face was followed by a fleeting reflective look, and Tom knew that he had asked for too little—possibly much too little, just as John had warned him.

'But now, Mr Cochrane! Five thousand pounds! *Pre*posterous!'

Balldragon showed all his teeth in a pained smile. 'Let me tell you this, Mr Cochrane. I have information that you accompanied Dr Stewart on a day following a certain ceilidh, at Invergarry. Very early in the day I believe. This was on one of my boats, *my* boats, Mr Cochrane. I have more than a suspicion that those pictures were taken from one of *my* boats. There was a picture—as I recall the fifth in the sequence—which showed the superstructure quite clearly. And you have the gall to stand there and seek to charge me five thousand pounds for pictures taken from my own boat! Come now, Mr Cochrane, let us have a little more realism.'

'I recognize the importance you attach to the boat, Dr Balldragon and, being a fair-minded man, I attach just as much importance to it being *your* boat as you do yourself. Otherwise my price would have been ten thousand.'

Balldragon grimaced again, showed his teeth, and at length gave a resigned shrug. Opening a desk drawer he took out a cheque-book. A moment later he handed Tom his draft for £5,000. After checking that the ink was dry, Tom folded it and placed it in his breast pocket and solemnly handed over a set of slides showing the Kelpie swimming just once around the boat.

'Susie, will you . . .'

Despina appeared in the doorway.

'Susie, will you show Mr Cochrane out?'

Tom drove immediately to the Royal Hibernian Bank, thinking the cheque should be cleared straight away. On the face of it Balldragon might stop it and yet keep the pictures, claiming they were taken from his boat, thus the property of L.N.R. But on reflection Tom thought not, because of the peculiar circumstances of the bargain. Balldragon believed he was buying an ingenious fake. Of course he wanted to use the pictures commercially as the genuine article, so he couldn't risk Tom's coming forward and exposing them as fake. It followed therefore that the cheque would be honoured.

It was strange that Tom for his part had been inhibited against asking a still higher price just because the pictures were genuine. After all, the monster existed. Somebody else might come along tomorrow with another fistful of pictures. Then the value would be gone. Tom found himself chuckling aloud as he walked into the bank. He wondered if there had ever been a bargain quite like this before, with the buyer thinking he was acquiring a fake, and the vendor knowing he was selling the genuine thing.

CHAPTER SEVEN

THE OFFICIAL PARTY

With the cheque deposited Tom spent an hour or so buying provisions before putting a personal call through to John at the physics lab. After what seemed an endless wait he came on the line, to inform Tom that he would be returning to Invermoriston on the following day.

This put Tom in a bit of a quandary. He didn't want to spend a day kicking his heels at Loch Ness. After actually sighting the Kelpie this would be an impossible anticlimax. So he spent the rest of the day in the Black Isle. A farmer out there was selling off a small farmhouse which Tom had a notion to buy. In past years ten acres of land went with the house, land which grew some of the best porridge oats in the country. The farmer of course wanted the land not the house, while Tom wanted both. He didn't want to farm it himself, being quite content to rent it out. So the situation was complex, involving much bargaining. Five thousand pounds would more than make the difference, Tom thought. This was why he'd fixed on that amount. He grinned to himself as he rumbled along. It was an ill Kelpie that blew nobody any good.

The following morning Tom drove back through Inverness. An evening of discussion had still left his negotiations complex and uncertain, but he had the distinct feeling that he was getting on top of the business.

The roadside along Loch Ness was full of blossom, and the day was fine, as it was every morning, which made the suddenness and ferocity of the storms even more remarkable and obscure.

There was little likelihood John would be back so early in the day, but nevertheless Tom stopped at the L.N.R. camp site just in case. Drawing a blank, as he'd expected, Tom drove on to Invermoriston, still debating what to do. It was then that he saw three vessels standing offshore. They were obviously at just about the size limit the Laggan locks could accommodate. One was a yacht, the other two were small naval gunboats. Tom, now curious, pulled the Land-Rover into the hotel car park and bounded into the hall. Here he heard a great commotion from the bar. A party of considerable size was singing with considerable animation the ribald shanty 'Oh, the Jolly Roger, Oh!'

'What the hell's going on, Kirste?' asked Tom of a girl who was hurrying towards the kitchen.

'They're looking to tear the place apart, Mr Cochrane,' said the wide-eyed Kirste from the isle of Eigg.

Whatever the intention, Tom wasn't going to be left out of such a party. He opened the bar door and strode firmly ahead in spite of the earth-shaking din. It was a sailor's party, so much was obvious. Then Tom saw, standing with his back to the bar conducting the incredible cats' chorus, the Prime Minister. The 'Oh, Jolly Roger, Oh!' came to a resounding climax as Tom eventually shouldered his way to the edge of the bar.

'A pint please,' he boomed above the last note of the song, and something in the resonance of his voice caught the P.M.'s ear.

'Ah, my friend from Edinburgh!' exclaimed the P.M., putting down his beer mug which he'd been using as a baton, 'Lads, this is the chap who advised us to come here.'

'Then buy the man a drink,' came a dozen voices in chorus.

The P.M. grabbed a tankard which the barman had just drawn, handed it to Tom, and pushed his own empty one back across the bar.

'Top that up, barman. This meeting deserves a toast. Lads, Tom Cochrane.'

'Tom Cochrane.'

'Have you sighted the monster yet?' asked Tom.

'No monster, but a damned great squall, just as we were coming into the loch.'

'A squall you say?'

'Real oceanic stuff.'

'Force 8,' remarked a young naval lieutenant.

'There was nothing in Inverness. I suppose this would have been early today wouldn't it?' asked Tom.

'Hellish early. Damned funny too, the way the boat rocked,' the P.M. went on.

'How funny?'

'Well it was as if . . .' began one of the yacht's crew, and then held up in mid-sentence.

'I know,' Tom continued, 'as if a giant hand had rocked the boat.'

'Exactly,' agreed the P.M., 'as if a giant hand had rocked the boat. Damned strange.'

'Never had it like that before. Not even in the Tasman,' said another of the crew.

A studious looking young naval officer came into the bar carrying a fistful of papers.

'Buy old swot-box a drink, sir,' yelled the chorus.

Then the expression on the lad's face quietened them. He came towards the P.M. clutching his papers. 'It's queer, sir,' he began. 'We got impulses on our electronic gear—during the storm.'

'Impulses! Should damned well think we did. Almost threw me overboard,' roared the P.M.

'I don't mean that, sir. I mean these impulses have a kind of regular beat to them.'

'That's just what we were saying, as if . . .' began Tom.

'A giant hand had rocked the boat,' concluded the P.M.

'Take a look, sir. You can see it all on the pen-chart records,' went on the young lieutenant.

The P.M. followed the lieutenant's finger as he traced it over the paper. Tom managed to see over the P.M.'s shoulder. Sure enough there did appear to be a kind of regular pattern to it.

'Taah ra-ra-ra-ra ra ra rat tah,' muttered the P.M., 'repeated four times. Then a lot more mixed up stuff.'

'What's that, sir?' asked one of the crew.

'Taah ra-ra-ra-ra ra ra rat tah,' repeated the P.M. a little faster than before. Everybody started with 'Taah ra-ra-ra-ra ra ra rat taah.'

'Sounds vaguely reminiscent of some musical phrase,' added the P.M., still using his tankard as a baton.

Tom couldn't forbear singing out the phrase in his rich voice. 'Taah ra-ra-ra-ra ra ra rat taah.'

'Too slow,' grunted the P.M.

'We'd have been vomiting in doggy bags if it had gone any faster,' remarked a raffish, bearded lad.

'Sing it again.'

Tom really let loose the second time, putting in some melodic interpretation.

'Not right. Not fast enough. Not the right notes.'

Tom resisted the urge to tell the P.M. to sing it himself.

'If only we had a piano.'

'You're not going to play the whole bloody storm, sir?' asked another crew member in mock anxiety.

'There's a piano in the main lounge. Quite a good one too,' Tom remarked.

'Then let's go. Bring your beer, lads.'

The lounge was a long good-sized room. At one end was a medium grand piano. At the other end there were seats around a fireplace. When the party had walked, stumped and strolled its way from the bar, the P.M. fixed himself up on a stool at the piano. He began by striking out the rhythm without melodic interpretation, all on one note. He tried it both slow and fast. Then suddenly he shouted, 'I've got it!' and was off at a great pace. The taah ra-ra-ra-ra ra ra rat taah repeated four times, just as it did on the pen chart. Then the P.M. was thundering away on a fast passage which rose and fell, followed by a lot of rapid stuff in the left hand.

'Did we go through all that and still survive to tell the tale?' muttered the raffish character, a little green around the gills. It was three to four minutes before the P.M. desisted and in this time the taah ra-ra-ra-ra ra ra rat tah was repeated quite a number of times.

'Beethoven. Opus 2 Number 3. First movement. When you see the score the ra-ra-ra-ra looks like thirds but really it's a double trill.'

He repeated the opening phrase. Then he repeated a passage in rapidly rising broken octaves. 'They say Beethoven could play those octaves with his first and little fingers. I wish I could,' he concluded.

'You must have a very good memory, sir,' said Tom.

'I've been practising this piece quite a bit lately as it happens.'

There was a pause.

'Lately!' repeated Tom, his jollity suddenly clouded by an unknown fear.

'Well, there isn't any doubt about it, is there? I mean it's the same as the pen chart.'

'Yes, it's the same all right. That's the strange part, the pen chart being just the same as the piece you've been practising lately, Prime Minister.'

The P.M. got up from the stool. 'I see what you mean,' he muttered, then walked the length of the room deep in thought.

At this precise moment the door was flung open. Standing there was Despina, without the grey wig. Her hair was dark brown, black almost. She advanced to the centre of the room, as if taking stage directions, and announced sepulchrally in her deep voice, 'Dr Ball-dragon is no more.'

'I beg your pardon, madam?' said the P.M.

Despina continued to stare dead straight ahead, as if

in a trance. But apparently she heard the P.M. for she repeated now with a tremor in her voice, 'Dr Balldragon is no more.' Then she collapsed, sobbing violently.

'Get her a stiff whisky, a very stiff whisky,' Tom said to the raffish character.

The whisky soon appeared. It took a little time before they had Despina coughing and spluttering. Slowly in gulps and snatches they got the story from her. She began by pointing an accusing finger at Tom. She told how he, Tom, had brought pictures of the monster to her employer, Balldragon, and how the good doctor had bought them. If it hadn't been for that, she moaned, the good doctor would still at this very moment be alive and well. They all turned to Tom, who without more ado filled in his side of the story.

'Five thousand pounds. That's what the good doctor paid for them,' shouted Despina.

'More fool him,' muttered the Prime Minister.

Tom reached into his pocket, took out the slide box, extracted a transparency, and handed it to the P.M.

'You say this thing is genuine?' asked the P.M. after a careful study.

'It certainly is.'

The others in the room started clamouring, so Tom allowed the single picture to circulate, doubting he would ever see it again.

Tom was eventually able to piece together what had happened to Balldragon. According to Despina, who was a bit more coherent now, Balldragon had become very puzzled by the pictures. He had gone out on the loch himself, presumably to check the background to the pictures. Somehow the boat had overturned and the unfortunate Balldragon drowned.

Had the good doctor gone alone, they asked the wretched woman. No, he'd gone with one of his employees, a certain David Robinson, and it was he who had managed to reach the shore, babbling about a monster with a snake-like neck which overturned their boat and dragged the struggling Balldragon to the depths of the loch. Tom bore Balldragon no ill will, especially after the five thousand pounds, but it seemed to him the most ironic death imaginable—to be dragged to the loch bottom by the monster whose *bona fides* one refused to recognize.

'I think this is something we should look into ourselves,' Tom heard the P.M. say.

'Aye, aye, sir!' came the chorus.

So without hesitation they left the room. The intention was plainly to go out on the loch to search for the missing Balldragon, or alternatively to search for clues to the manner of his passing.

Tom wanted to attach himself to the party, but he first had to check and see if John had returned. He felt he would have plenty of time to get to the L.N.R. camp site and back before the crews organized themselves.

John had indeed returned. There was a note to say so, but no sign of the Viking himself. Tom's immediate desire was to rush back and join the hunt, but common sense told him that he was hardly likely to get a view of the Monster half as good as before. He also wanted to hear what John had been up to, which meant in rational terms remaining where he was.

Tom sat around for half an hour before he saw the shooting brake hammering towards him.

'Hi!' shouted John with a wave of the hand as it drew up alongside.

The question now was who should talk first. Tom decided to fill John in on the P.M.'s party, which he did in less than a hundred words.

'You mean they've gone out on the loch?' asked John when Tom was finished.

'That's right.'

'Bloody fools! We must stop them.'

'They'll be away by now.'

'We can try.'

Tom responded to this astonishing reaction by jumping into the brake.

'O.K. Drive like the wind then. Some of them were pretty well sozzled. So perhaps they're still messing about. We may be able to stop 'em.'

On reaching Invermoriston the boats were gone. They could see them in the distance, moving out, away from the shore.

'Bloody fools,' yelled John, waving his arms in desperate resignation.

CHAPTER EIGHT

CREATURE IN THE LOCH

There was no calling the boats back, so Tom and John made their way to the caravan.

'Well, what's new,' began Tom. 'What have you discovered?'

John took out a sheet of paper from his briefcase and laid it on a table.

Loch	D/H (Per cent)	
	Top water	Bottom water
Tay	0·0147	0·0132
Ericht	0·0148	0·0132
Arkaig	0·0150	0·0135
Morar	0·0149	0·0142
Quoich	0·0149	0·0143
Mullardoch	0·0147	0·0103
Ordinary Sea Water	0·0152	—
Tap water	0·0150	—
Ness	0·0149	0·0069

'D means deuterium,' explained John, 'the form of hydrogen present in heavy water.'

'The atomic energy stuff?'

'Right, the material physicists are trying to make into helium.'

'This I presume is the ratio of heavy water to ordinary water,' said Tom prodding the second and third columns.

'Right. As fractions of a per cent.'

'Why the differences?'

'That's exactly the problem. Why the differences? There's very little in the top water but notice the differences in the bottom water. The usual range for sea water is from about 0·150 to 0·152, a pretty narrow variation. The range is wider for ordinary rain water, from about 0·0144 to 0·0152. You'll see the top water from every loch falls into this range,'

'But the bottom water is much lower.'

'That's partly because snow has a lower value, from something like 0·0108 to 0·145.'

'I see. The bottom water, being cold, has come mostly from melting snow.'

'Right, And it's lower for Tay and Ericht, because they get more snow water than Morar and Quoich.'

'How about Ness? That's way out of line with the others.'

'Which is exactly the sixty-four thousand dollar question. It's miles outside the possible tolerances, even for snow.'

'Well, the top water and bottom water haven't been mixed, that's pretty conclusive,' nodded Tom, realizing this was what John was so excited about. 'Which brings us back to the temperature problem,' he added.

'Not so fast. Forget the temperature problem for a

minute. How could the D/H get as low as 0·0069? Let's tackle that question first.'

'I suppose you can't have special snow?'

John laughed derisively, 'There's just one way to get a ratio as low as 0·0069. That's to take D out of the water. Somehow D is being taken out of the bottom water of Loch Ness.'

Tom sat for a long time studying the table. 'I suppose there's no possibility of a mistake?' he asked at length.

'I wish there were. I blasted well wish there were. Although there's a discrepancy I don't understand. I'd be a bit more comfortable with my theory if Morar was low as well. But you'll see that it's Mullardoch which is low, not Morar.'

'Mullardoch!' queried Tom, mindful of the freak storm on Beinn Fhionnliadh.

'My theory,' John hesitated, 'is that something— some creature—is separating D, separating it to produce energy for converting it to helium. Heat must be produced and lost in the conversion process. That's the reason for the bottom water being more than two degrees higher than it should be. Heat loss from helium synthesis.'

John looked hard at Tom, who just stared back. 'It adds up', said Tom breaking the silence, 'except I don't see the Kelpie in the role of a nuclear scientist.'

'The Kelpie is something different,' said John defensively.

'You're not telling me we're dealing with two creatures?'

'Yes and no. The Kelpie was *made* by the creature on the bottom of the loch.'

212

'Made?' boomed Tom.

'The Kelpie is a telepuppet.'

'A what?'

'A telepuppet. Look, you know this vehicle the Russians have landed on the Moon. They drive it around, don't they? Well the point is that the driver can be back here on the Earth, so long as the vehicle is equipped with television cameras for eyes. If the cameras are good enough, the driver—here on Earth—can tell if there are obstacles ahead.'

'And instruct the vehicle to go round 'em,' concluded Tom.

'Yes, almost like driving an ordinary car.'

'You're telling me the Kelpie isn't a thing of flesh and blood at all. It's a swimming machine, equipped inside with electronics?'

'Right!' exclaimed John decisively.

'This needs thinking about,' muttered Tom, spying a packet of biscuits and taking one. 'Suppose you were down there on the loch bottom and suppose you were as clever as a barrel of monkeys. It's reasonable to assume you'd want to take a look at the world above the surface of the water. What would one do? You could put up some kind of periscope.'

'Seven hundred feet long?' interposed John, shaking his head.

'I know. It would be clumsy. So instead you'd make a swimming machine,' went on Tom his mouth full of biscuit.

'It figures.'

Tom suddenly started to chuckle. 'So when the Kelpie was swimming around our boat, and I was taking pictures, all the time it was taking pictures of us. I wonder if it got five thousand quid for 'em?'

'How much water is there in Loch Ness?' asked John, frowning at Tom's hilarity.

'A powerful lot.'

'All right, how much?'

'Got some paper?' said Tom helping himself to another biscuit.

Tom set about the problem. He remembered he'd estimated the area of Loch Ness to be about forty square miles. He pencilled down the figure of a thousand million square feet. Multiplying by about six hundred feet for the average depth, he got roughly six hundred thousand million cubic feet of water. Now one cubic foot weighed 62 pounds. So by multiplying by 62, and dividing by 2,240, Tom worked out the approximate mass in tons.

'Roughly twenty thousand million tons.'

'I'd prefer it in grams,' said John. 'Twenty thousand million tons are $2 \cdot 10^{16}$ grams. Let's count a half of that as bottom water, 10^{16} grams. Now let's see how much D has been taken out. First, we notice that 10^{16} grams of water means about 10^{15} grams of hydrogen, in one form or another. If $0 \cdot 014$ per cent of this was D to start with, then the original amount, before any separation, was $1 \cdot 4 \times 10^{11}$ grams. O.K.?'

'I think so,' said Tom, running his eye over the figures.

'Roughly a half of the D has been taken out, probably a bit less than half. So, conservatively we arrive at $5 \cdot 10^{10}$ grams for the amount taken out.'

'What's all this in aid of?'

'Suppose the D has been converted to helium. What sort of an energy yield do we arrive at? Well, one gram of D yields about $6 \cdot 10^{18}$ ergs, so $5 \cdot 10^{10}$ grams yields $3 \cdot 10^{29}$ ergs.'

Tom's whistle was loud and shrill. He knew that burning a ton of coal or oil gave about 10^{18} ergs. So this thing was producing as much heat as three hundred thousand million tons of oil. This was a hundred times more than the amount of oil burnt in a year throughout the world. It was vast, almost beyond comprehension.

The sky had grown very dark during their calculations. Outside everything was uncannily still. There wasn't a ripple on the loch, and no wind stirred the grasses along the roadside.

'How would all this energy show itself?' asked Tom.

'That's quite a problem.'

'Heating the water?'

'Why heat the water?'

'Maybe to reach some optimum temperature. Perhaps it's too cold for the creature's liking.'

'Could be, I suppose. The difficulty is you don't need anything like that amount of energy, just to heat the water. Lifting the temperature by two degrees only needs 10^{24} ergs.'

Tom jotted figures down on his piece of paper.

He soon found John's answer to be spot on.

'Why have a potentiality for more than 10^{29} ergs if you're only in need of 10^{24} ergs. That's what I can't understand?' John shook his head in puzzlement. 'It looks more as if the heating was a by-product. But even then whatever process the thing uses must be very efficient. To get more than 10^{29} ergs, with a heat loss of only 10^{24} ergs, would be fantastically efficient.'

Suddenly there was a brilliant flash. Both men braced themselves for the ensuing peal of thunder. Five, ten, twenty seconds went by and still no noise. The loch was smooth and the grasses still. The first flash was followed by others, with increasing rapidity, until the outside world was full of light.

Then the rain fell. Not a shower, or a heavy storm, but an unprecedented deluge of monsoon proportions. Just as suddenly the loch was whipped into motion by a gale force wind which bent the trees at creaking angles.

The storm on Beinn Fhionnliadh had been something quite out of the ordinary in Tom's memory, but this was worse in order of magnitude. An idea which had been forming in his mind burst forth, but he was unable to communicate with John, partly because of the noise of the wind, and partly because water was now pouring into the caravan through the faulty roof. The wind strength was so enormous that, as they shifted the more essential items from one end of the van to the other, they could feel the floor heave as though some creature were pushing on the side of the van in an effort to turn them over.

The storm stopped with a suddenness which was almost as unnerving as its beginning. An explosive upward current of air violently dissipated the dense black clouds, allowing sunlight to penetrate once again to ground level. The heat lifted a thin veil from the grassy bank outside the van. On stepping outside, the two men found the air was soft and humid, like the inside of a greenhouse.

'What do you think?' asked John.

'The worst. We'd better get on over to the hotel.'

'How substantial is the Prime Minister's boat?' asked John as he set the vehicle in motion.

'God only knows. Not much will have come through that last lot.'

John braked the car to a stop outside the hotel. Tom was just pulling on the door latch when he caught a glimpse of the end wall, the one facing the loch. He climbed slowly out and stood staring at the hotel. There on the wall, some fifteen feet across, in full colour, shining in the sparkling sun, was a portrait of Dr Balldragon.

CHAPTER NINE

THE WHIRLWIND

'Jumping Jehosophat,' exclaimed John, 'It's Ball-dragon.'

The two men walked up to the wall.

'Fused. Into a kind of glass,' muttered Tom.

'How about the colours?'

'Impurities in the glass, I suppose.'

'But how was it done?'

Tom simply shook his head. This astonishing event more or less disposed of a theory he'd been developing. But it suggested other still more remarkable ideas, so remarkable that Tom continued standing there, shaking his head.

'Better find out if anyone knows anything about it,' Tom said after an interval.

They walked a few steps towards the hotel entrance. The sound of an approaching car from the direction of Fort Augustus caught Tom's attention. It couldn't be, he thought, but it was Flora's prestige car, with Jeannie at the wheel.

'Oh, so you're here,' said Flora as the two women climbed from the car.

'You'd better come and take a look at what we've found,' said John. Might give Flora something to occupy her mind, thought Tom as he brought up the rear of the procession.

Jeannie let out a scream, but Flora looked up at the portrait for a while, 'It's beautiful. Like the Rosette Window at Chartres,' she commented.

Indeed the colouring in the glass sparkled in the warm sunlight. Tom marvelled at the working of his wife's mind. She simply saw glass, sparkling and shining. It never occurred to her to ask how the picture was done, why it had been plastered across the wall, or who Balldragon was. No doubt she thought it to be the latest gimmick of the local brewery company.

A loud exclamation behind them sent Tom revolving to find Kirste, the girl from Eigg, standing there her hand to her mouth.

'Who is it, sir?'

'This is the good doctor. The one drowned by the Kelpie.'

'Oh no!' shouted the girl, running towards the hotel entrance. But too late. Out came Despina. Kirste tried to head her off but Despina was in one of her floating moods, sailing serenely ahead, not noticing anything around her. Tom wondered if the woman suffered from short sight. His uncertainty on this point lasted only seconds. Despina half turned her head towards the end wall, then swung round in a convulsive jerk, gave an extremely loud, piercing shriek, and fainted into John's arms.

Flora was in her element now. She had John carry Despina to the grass verge.

'Get her head down. Down!' she commanded.

Meantime Tom was finding out from Kirste what had happened during the last storm.

'It came all over the hotel,' the girl said.

'What did?'

'This river of fire. It was like a river, sir, rolling over everything. All colours. It had all colours and very bright.'

All colours, that was just what Willie Ferguson had said. At least Tom knew now how the stone at the end of the hotel had been fused, for it was clear that a fireball—like the one Willie Ferguson had seen—had passed directly over the hotel. The picture of Balldragon was something else. Tom didn't understand that, but at least it explained the dead forester, the poor fellow in the ride among the trees above Loch Lochy. The forester had been electrocuted by another such fireball.

There were shouts from the direction of the lochside. Tom left Despina in the care of Flora and John and made his way to the little jetty. In relief of the apprehension he'd begun to feel, he could see the Prime Minister's yacht on its way back, some half-mile from the shore. Oddly enough, there were no accompanying gunboats. This was strange. So too was the complete absence of noise and demonstration with which the crew anchored the yacht and ferried themselves ashore. They made their way in silence, in contrast with their former rumbustious behaviour. Tom studied their white expressionless faces. Quite a picnic, he thought. Still it was a relief to see the Prime Minister safe and sound. The P.M. made his way slowly to the hotel, a sodden, bedraggled figure. He disappeared through the main entrance, apparently without noticing Balldragon's astonishing portrait.

Tom examined the picture more dispassionately than he'd been able to do so far. He felt the colouring was quite remarkably faithful, at any rate so far as he could remember from his one meeting with the doctor. Somewhere in his subconscious it reminded him of something. He continued to gaze at the astonishing effigy as he racked his mind for an answer.

Flora nudged his arm.

'Well, what is it?' he asked.

'You can get my bags out of the car.'

'You're staying here?'

'Of course.'

Tom found the usual plethora of luggage which Flora always took around with her. Unceremoniously he stuffed a bag under each arm and grabbed a suitcase in each hand. Then he remembered who it was that the effigy reminded him of, the Coachman in Disney's Pinocchio.

On his last trip to the prestige car he encountered John coming up the stairs as he was dropping down.

'I thought the P.M. might like a stiff tot,' John explained, waving a bottle of rum.

'He probably would but you can't go barging in,' said Tom in some surprise.

'What happened to those gunboats?' came the reply.

'I don't know.'

'Weren't they here to protect him?'

'I suppose so.'

'Well, they wouldn't just leave him.'

'No.'

'I'd like to find out what happened,' said John with immense authority and confidence.

'Curiosity killed the cat.'

'It's not going to kill me. Coming? The girl told me

it was the second room on the right, down the corridor to the left. Sounds topologically complicated.'

Tom followed behind John, who rapped good and firmly on what he judged to be the appropriate bedroom door, then elected to interpret a muffled shout as an invitation to enter. Reluctant but fascinated, Tom tagged on behind. The main bedroom was empty but there were vague sounds of splashing coming from the connecting bathroom.

'After that soaking, I'll bet he's as cold as a witch's tit,' remarked John.

They'd waited for the best part of a quarter of an hour when suddenly the connecting door was flung open and the P.M. came stalking out wearing a dressing-gown.

'Yes, what is it?' he asked stiffly.

'I thought you might like a warming drink, sir,' responded John, brandishing his bottle.

'I might, but I could have asked for it myself.'

'I appreciate that you may not wish to be disturbed, sir, but we have some information which I think you would want to know about.'

'Information! What information?'

'I'll pour you a drink first, sir, because it's quite a story and it'll take a little while to tell.'

With magnificent confidence John marched into the bathroom, returning a few seconds later with a glass.

'Are you in on this?' asked the Prime Minister, looking at Tom.

'Yes, Prime Minister. I think you should hear what Dr Stewart has to say.'

John launched his discourse with a description of

how he'd found the temperature of the bottom water of Loch Ness to be too high. He went on with an account of how Tom had confirmed this to be so, of how the deuterium content of the bottom water was much too low. He concluded with the deductions that followed this discovery.

'What it comes down to is that this enormous energy output, $3 \cdot 10^{29}$ ergs, is as much as the yield from a million H-bombs. You've been out there this afternoon, Prime Minister, sailing on top of a kind of silo with a million H-bombs inside it.'

The Prime Minister was thoughtful for several moments. Then he turned to Tom.

'How do you see this business, Mr Cochrane?'

'I agree with most of what Dr Stewart has said.'

'You don't agree with everything?'

'There's one gap in the argument. Granted the deuterium has been separated—fifty per cent of it separated—we still don't have definite knowledge of its being converted to helium.'

'The water temperature?'

'Only a little would be needed. I think the storms are more significant than the water temperature.'

'The storms?' There was a hard look on the P.M.'s face now.

'It can hardly be doubted that these storms are artificial. They're connected with the loch, with something in the loch.'

'You mean there could be a form of energy dissipation much bigger than the water temperature?' asked John.

'Yes, because in a storm it's the latent heat of

223

evaporation of water which matters. This might need a hundred times more energy than would be required for heating the water alone.'

'All this is somehow connected with what happened this afternoon, I suppose,' began the P.M.

'What did happen this afternoon?' asked Tom.

'It's a little difficult. Well, we made our way out there in a pretty cheerful mood. You saw us leave, Mr Cochrane.'

'Yes.'

'Then the storm hit us. It was a really bad one. But I'm used to bad weather. At least I thought I was, until the black wall came at us.'

'What was that?'

'A whirlwind. The air was moving so fast the motion of it seemed black. Not just dark, black.'

'Please go on.'

'It came at us, straight on.'

'Good God,' muttered Tom.

'The escort was ahead. The whirlwind swept over them like an express train. By the grace of God it took a hop and lifted as it came over the yacht. I've heard stories about people who've been in the very throat of a whirlwind. That's just what happened to us. We were able to look up from the very middle of it.'

'What did you see?'

'It was like a huge cavern with dark walls. There was a deep hum, like a vast cosmic dynamo. I saw the escort vessels ripped to pieces, then tossed high in the air. In the odd second or two the wreckage must have been lifted from maybe five hundred feet to a thousand or more.'

'You mean they're gone!' burst out John.

'Gone, gone!' There was a wild look about the P.M. 'But I'm going to do something about it. If what you say is right, if there really is something happening, on this loch bottom, then we'll give it something to think about. With the biggest depth-charges we've got!'

'But, sir!' began John.

'But what?'

'I think my young friend was going to advise caution, Prime Minister.'

'Caution!'

'On the grounds that this phenomenon may be exceedingly powerful.'

'We shall see.'

'The risk could be enormous,' John protested.

'It could, but the risk now is enormous. Tell me, what would be the risk in dropping high explosives into a silo of H-bombs? Very little, I imagine.'

'This could be different.'

'It was you, young man, who used the analogy of a silo.'

The Prime Minister walked a few steps to a phone. As he took it from the cradle, he indicated by a nod towards the outer door that he wished to be alone. Tom and John withdrew. Outside Tom turned to John.

'You shouldn't have given him that stiff rum.'

'I guess not. Shock and rum . . .'

'He won't do anything without consulting his Chief of Staff.'

'Anything in that?'

'Well, they're not likely to bomb unless there's a consensus.'

'Sure enough there'll be a consensus.'

'Then there's nothing we can do about it,' muttered Tom. 'Let's go down by the loch. I've got an idea,' he added.

The two men walked out onto the jetty. Tom took a pencil stub and a grubby piece of paper from his pocket.

'I've been wondering about draining the loch,' he announced.

'That's a hell of an idea.'

'Is it really as daft as it sounds? Supposing we had all the pumps and pipes we needed. How big a pipe could we get?'

'Ten-foot radius, maybe.'

Tom began the kind of arithmetical calculation he loved.

'Ten-foot radius gives a cross-section area of about 300 square feet. Suppose we had really powerful pumps with a flow of 10 feet per second. The outflow from the pipe would be 3,000 cubic feet a second.'

He paused for a moment while calculating and then went on, 'I make the outflow to be about 100 tons a second. This afternoon we had twenty thousand million tons for the whole loch, didn't we?'

'Right.'

'So it would take two hundred million seconds to empty the loch.'

'About seven years,' interposed John with a grimace.

'That's not so bad, for just one pipe. We could have lots of outlet pipes. With ten of 'em, the job could be done in less than a year.'

'How about the inflow?'

'Well the rivers and all the burns would have to be diverted to the other side of the locks at the ends. It would be awkward but not hard, really.'

John was becoming more interested now. The thought of finding out what was happening on the loch bottom was beginning to fascinate him.

'There's obviously no pressure problem on the lock gates at the ends. Pumps could lift the water all right, but how much energy would be needed?'

Tom began more calculations.

'Well in grams we had $2 \cdot 10^{16}$ for the whole lot. Lifting each gram by an average of shall we say 100 metres would need—what? 10^7 ergs?'

'I reckon.'

'So we get $2 \cdot 10^{23}$ ergs needed. Two hundred thousand tons of coal or oil.'

'About a million barrels of oil?'

'Not an absurd amount, considering what might be at stake,' Tom concluded.

Both men continued to gaze out across the loch, both wondering what would be found should the waters be suddenly parted and the bottom revealed.

CHAPTER TEN

THE BOMBING OF THE LOCH

In the ensuing three days there was a great deal of activity in and around Loch Ness. First there came an invasion of the area by military intelligence, who then proceeded to direct immediate operations from Fort Augustus. Next the road along the Great Glen was closed to all except those with official passes, hastily supplied to the local population. Communication across the Great Glen was limited to the Glenfinnan–Mallaig road in the south and to the A9 through Inverness in the north. This permitted all visitors to the north-west to make their way back to their homes in the south, although it was a long frustrating trip on the crowded narrow roads.

All hamlets fringing Loch Ness were evacuated. Preparations were set in hand even to evacuate Fort Augustus if need be. Invermoriston was wholly taken over by the military as their advanced base. H.Q. was established, not at Fort Augustus, but at the hotel in Tomdoun, a quiet spot off the tourist route to Skye. It was to Tomdoun that the Prime Minister moved, and John with Jeannie.

It was somewhat natural for John to become attached to the H.Q. party, for he was the person with technical knowledge, who knew the details. He'd preserved water samples. These were taken to Government laboratories in England. Analysis soon confirmed the abnormal D/H ratio for the bottom water of Loch Ness. This gave John real status among the top brass, which he enjoyed.

Tom could have managed to attach himself to the H.Q. party if he'd wanted to, but he hadn't. The morning following the loss of the gunboats, Flora started away towards Inverness, leaving Tom with the impression she'd gone back to Edinburgh. He spent the better part of the day checking all his camping gear and repacking the Land-Rover so that the essential items he needed were at hand. He made a journey to Fort Augustus specially to acquire a new cylinder of bottle gas. On his return to Invermoriston he found that Flora had reappeared, her car chock-a-block with foods of all kinds.

Tom and Flora argued for some little time over his suggestion that she should join Jeannie at H.Q., but Flora would have none of it. So there he was, stuck with her.

He informed the military that he and Flora were going over to Kintail. After considerable argument, for his temper was rising, he was given a pass, but only after he threatened reference to the P.M. The pass required him to check with military intelligence at Kintail, which he had no intention of doing.

Tom started off on the Dalchreichart – Cluanie – Kintail road. They took both vehicles. Before Dalchreichart they crossed Torgyle Bridge to the south side of the river and then cut back east for about a mile to another bridge across a large burn. Here they turned sharp right up a forestry road, which took them steeply upwards through thick trees for another mile. Flora had a lot of trouble in the prestige car, but with the aid of a couple of tows from the Land-Rover they managed at last to reach the upper edge of the wood. This satisfied Tom. He had no wish to have lightning bringing down trees on top of them, yet he needed the wood to shield them from the prying eyes of the military.

The camp he set up was situated on the flanks of the western containing wall of the Great Glen itself. In case John was right about the explosive powers hidden in the loch, he had the hill between himself and the water. He would need to walk uphill for about seven hundred feet before he could look down on the Great Glen, and he would then need to travel north-east for some three miles before he could look down on Loch Ness itself.

In fact, after a meal, he left Flora to her own devices and walked to a strategic spot which gave him an excellent view up the whole length of Loch Ness. It was a spot about three miles south-west of Inver-moriston and about three miles north of Fort Augustus.

The bombing raids began the following day. Sorties of planes flew low along the Great Glen in the direction south-west to north-east. Tom was abroad early. Much to his surprise Flora was up shortly afterwards. He prepared a couple of Thermos flasks of tea before they set off up the hillside and along the ridge, arriving at the spot Tom had chosen the previous evening by about 7.30 a.m. From here they could watch the planes coming up the Great Glen.

The depth-charges made a kerroomph on explosion,

throwing up plumes of water. At a distance of more than three miles the white columns looked small and the sound of the explosions weak. Nothing like the roar of recent storms.

Tom had half expected another storm, but the weather remained fine with nothing to suggest the strange events of the past couple of weeks, which in a way made the exercise they were watching absurd. It appeared a case of much-ado-about-nothing. The rest of the day was spent therefore in following pursuits of their own. One bird watching, the other reading.

In a dozen messes throughout the country air-force officers were congratulating themselves on a wizard show. The depth-charges had made a most satisfactory kerroomph. Often enough before they'd flown along the valley of the Scottish Highlands but never before on an actual operation. Ops made all the difference.

At about the same time TV in the U.S. had amusingly shown those quaint folk, the British, bombing the hell out of their traditional monster, the monster of Loch Ness. St George and the Dragon all over again. On the other hand a certain U.S. citizen, J. J. Stewart, had been mightily relieved to have the day pass without serious incident. It never occurred to John that his idea on the nature of Loch Ness might be wholly wrong— but the idea had certainly occurred by now to members of the Prime Minister's staff.

Tom had to admit to himself that the day had been uneventful, even boring. He'd gone up to his hill camp in a high spirit of adventure. All the excitement he'd had was listening to the incessant roar and boom of high-speed aircraft. Even the bird-watching had been unsatisfactory with the disturbance of the birds by the explosions. So at the end of the day, while Flora climbed happily into the front of the Land-Rover, Tom forced his body into the small tent, still grumbling to himself about the wasted day.

Tom woke about 1 a.m. It was pretty much the way it had been the night of the first freak storm, the night before he'd discovered the body of the electrocuted forester. Very heavy rain. Feeling things were likely to get worse, knowing water would eventually flow into the tent, Tom put on his clothes, grabbed his sleeping-bag and made a dash for Flora's car. He stubbed his toes in the dark. Cursing loudly he scrambled inside and slammed the door. It wasn't easy to stretch himself out, so he resigned himself to sitting half upright for the rest of the night, or at any rate until the storm abated.

But the storm did not abate. The heavy rain became a deluge. It drummed violently on the metal roof. Tom could have sworn that it wasn't rain at all but waves breaking over the car, crashing down on the car. He began to fear for their safety. At least they could hardly be submerged. Being on a hillside, the torrent must rush past them down into the valley below. He pondered about the vehicles being swept away by the water but decided the hillside was too irregular for them to be moved very far.

Dawn was no more than a vague diffused light seeping through a sky of incredible blackness. Water raced downwards everywhere, not just in a few scattered burns. Tom felt it doubtful whether the bridge at the bottom would survive. When the main burn eventually subsided he could probably get the Land-Rover across and out to the main road, but it would be hopeless to attempt it with Flora's car.

Two more hours dragged by and still there was no remission in the fantastic downpour. The first freak storms had seemed incredible but they were merely curtain raisers to this one. He wondered how Flora was managing. Then he saw her trying to open the Land-Rover door. Tom dashed across the thirty yards or so, then heaved at the nearside door. Several times the wind almost knocked his feet from under him. Realizing there was little hope of getting it open, he started off round the side of the vehicle. The fury of the wind caught him and threw him like a bale of straw into the mud. For several minutes he lay there, head buried in the quagmire, unable to move. The rain stung the backs of his hands and his soaked body became cold, making his teeth chatter.

Using his arms as paddles he started inching his way forward to the door. Suddenly he saw the Land-Rover move. He waited for it to smash his body to pieces but it settled back on its wheels.

'What is it?' Flora asked as he hauled his limp body into the driver's seat.

'Rrrrain,' he said, flicking the ignition on and starting the engine. With low four-wheel drive he slithered the Land-Rover into the protection of the trees.

'What's causing it?' she said handing him a cup of steaming tea.

'I don't know.'

Tom marvelled at his wife's composure. An outrageous demand from a student committee would send her into high passion, but nothing in the natural world seemed capable of putting her out of countenance. Tom had the feeling she could be wheeled across Niagara Falls on a tightrope without noticing anything untoward. Comparison with Niagara might seem absurd, he thought, but the sheer volume of water coming down now, probably over hundreds of square miles, must be truly enormous. He finished his tea, stripped, and donned dry clothing.

When by 10 a.m. there was still no remission he decided he'd waited long enough. He pulled on all the waterproof clothing he could find.

'Where are you going?'

'Out.'

'Don't be absurd.'

'I want to find out what's going on.'

'Can't you see what's going on?' said Flora pointing through the window.

Deciding there was no profit in such a conversation, he carefully tied himself into his clothing so that the rain would have as little chance to penetrate to his body as possible. When everything was ready he forced his way out into the murky gloom.

Normally the walk to the hilltop would have taken less than half an hour. Today it took an eternity. He reached the hilltop because he was curious. His progress there looked like a drunk on his way home. Stumbling, crawling and falling he inched his way, using what cover was available to protect his bruised body from the ferocity of the wind.

The top wasn't a sharp crested ridge. It was a broad undulating plateau. After he'd recovered his wind, he looked around, disappointed there was nothing to see, except a black sky above, a wall of water in his face, and an endless boggy vegetation, which in this downpour was like a sea of green glue.

More difficult still was the object of this exercise. Three miles had still to be covered along the top plateau before there was any hope of seeing Loch Ness.

The water pounding Tom's head caused a feeling of concussion, like continuous mortar fire. The incessant thudding reduced his mental processes to shreds. He crawled and stumbled on, not caring. In his stupor Tom wondered how there could be so much ammunition up there in the sky. Then with the force of a twenty-five-pound shell his wandering mind clicked back into its groove. He hadn't been blown to the ground, he was walking standing up.

The wind was slackening. Tom moved steadily along the ridge, despite the ceaseless rain, checking his direction from time to time with a compass strapped to his wrist.

Near both mental and physical exhaustion, he at length reached the spot where yesterday they'd sat in the sunshine. Hard to believe it was only yesterday. Hard to believe it was the same place, even the same planet. In the direction of Loch Ness it was totally black.

Slowly the appalling truth dawned on Tom Cochrane. The waters of Loch Ness were being lifted into the air. The rain thundering down on his head was from Loch Ness. An enormous funnel of air was sucking the water up many thousands of feet. Some of it, perhaps most of it, seemed to be going right up into the high level atmospheric circulation. At the edges of the loch the water was spraying out sideways—it was this more or less peripheral effect that was flooding down on this particular hill-top several miles away to the south. God knows what it must be like to be in the main updraught. Tom forced himself not to turn and run. He watched the incredible spectacle for a few minutes, then set off back along the ridge, staggering under the weight of water that slashed at his back and head.

It never occurred to Tom that he might never make it back to camp. The fact that not one person in ten would have had the slightest hope of reaching safety under these conditions never crossed his mind. Years of walking the hills had taught him to keep going, making instinctively the multitude of small decisions on which safety depends.

For once Flora seemed pleased to see him back.

'What was the use of going out in this? You can't see anything,' she said while Tom struggled into dry clothes.

'It's wet,' he replied.

'Too wet for us to be here. We should be getting out.'

'I don't think we can.'

'Why not?'

'The bridge will be down.'

Flora thought about the bridge for a while.

'There's just one thing to be thankful for,' he went on.

'What?'

'All that food you bought.'

Tom set up the cooking equipment in the back of the Land-Rover and prepared a meal, for he was immensely hungry after the hours in the cold rain.

The thunderous drumming of water on the roof stopped abruptly. This was some time around 3 p.m. Flora got out to sniff the air.

'It's very bright over there,' she called out.

Sure enough when Tom reached Flora he could see it was bright towards the north-east, which was surprising considering that was the direction of Loch Ness.

'Better go up and take a look,' he said.

'You're just like a yo-yo. Up and down all the time.'

It was still bright when they reached the hill-top. This was still to the north-east: in contrast to the dull grey sky in the other directions. Tom thought a powerful updraught over Loch Ness must be punching a hole in the cloud layer. He and Flora continued to slosh their way along the ridge towards the vantage point overlooking the loch.

The light continued to brighten. They still had about a mile to go when Tom stopped and gazed along the ridge. He could see a profusion of colours now. A sudden thought and he was forging his way at maximum speed across the soggy ground. Flora followed as best she could, dropping farther and farther behind her rapidly moving husband.

While Flora professed a total disinterest in physical phenomena the real truth was that the physical world frightened her. She was intensely disturbed by things she didn't understand. So she professed to ignore them, like the pedestrian crossing a busy road gazing up at the sky.

Tom and Flora stood at the spot overlooking the loch. The sky above them today was sombre. So it was to the south and west, but the long view along the trench of Loch Ness was ablaze with light. Many thousands of brilliantly coloured spheres were rising from the bottom of the loch. Mostly they were rising high into the upper atmosphere but a few came away at lower altitudes, spreading themselves over the surrounding countryside.

Flora slipped her hand into Tom's as they stood staring at this incredible phenomenon.

Tom's mind was blank. The bright coloured spheres rising into the air for a while seemed beautiful to him, until his roving eyes noted there was now no water left in Loch Ness. Where water had been there was a deep dark gash. Steep cliffs dropped seven hundred feet from the old shore line to a remarkably flat bottom. The sides of the trench were appallingly rough. Hundreds of waterfalls plunged from burns directly to the loch bottom, casting rainbows as the light from the spheres caught their spray. Tom stood in awe, seeing for the first time the trench just as it was when the vast ice river gouged the Great Glen ten thousand years ago.

He gazed long at this vast black hole. He had the impression he was now looking down on an explosion pit of unprecedented size. He wondered if Fort Augustus had been evacuated in time to escape this holocaust.

A cry from Flora interrupted his thoughts. One of

the fireballs was floating above the hillside not more than a mile away. They retreated quickly to the shelter of a small rocky outcrop.

As they watched, the fireball ceased to be a sphere. It became a ring, more strictly a torus. At first the colour in the ring was dominated by red, but gradually the red tones faded and were replaced by a brilliant lilac. At the same time an intensely red spot appeared at the centre of the ring. The whole structure was perhaps two hundred feet across, assuming the object was a mile away. It was like an enormous coloured eye. Because the ring appeared more or less circular, Tom had the feeling that the eye was looking in their direction—or alternatively in the opposite direction—or maybe both ways at the same time.

An enormous lightning flash burst forth from the central red spot. It hit the ground half a mile away. Instantly a sheet of flame covered several thousand square yards of ground. Instantly too there was a strange hissing roar as a vast steam cloud erupted from the rain soaked hillside.

The flame moved towards them like a stupendous prairie fire. There was no point in running, for they could make negligible speed over the wet clinging ground. Tom peered over the outcrop of rocks at the approaching steam cloud. Then he noticed the lilac ring was no longer circular. At the same moment he heard the drone of a plane, probably a reconnaissance flight, he thought. The lilac ring became increasingly elliptical. Once again lightning stabbed out from the central red spot. Instantly it seemed, the drone stopped. The flash had gone singeing its way upwards through the sky. There was no thunder. So there had been no pre-existing electric field along the path taken by the flash. Tom had little doubt of the aircraft's fate, total atomization.

They waited in trepidation for the eye to turn back towards them, but it didn't. It just resumed its shape as a fireball. It floated slowly and smoothly for a while, then accelerated rapidly to enormous speed, ascending as it did so through the cloud layer above them.

Tom squeezed Flora's hot sweaty hand which was gripping his. He was surprised to find himself sick, faint and cold. Looking back again at the dark trench made him shiver violently. With sudden resolve he set out as firmly as he could towards the area of the fire. Once again Flora stumped along in the rear. Tom eventually stopped and stared over a region of bare rock. All the vegetation had been burnt away, even though there had been several feet of it. There were no charred remains of any kind. The rock itself had been fused and was still glowing hot. Tom put his arm over Flora's shoulder as they looked at the scar. Then they turned and descended in silence to their camp.

CHAPTER ELEVEN

THE WAR OF THE WORLDS

The death toll turned out to be least among the residents of the region around Loch Ness. Before the bombing they were already uneasy. The strange weather of the preceding weeks had unsettled them. And the arrival in strength of the military followed by depth charges dropped in such profusion into the loch showed plainly that something very serious was going on. When it was reported late on the evening of the bombing that the surface of the loch was boiling everywhere like water in a vast pan, the people of Fort Augustus had no hesitation in quitting their beds and homes and making off to what they considered a safe distance.

The shortest route away from the loch lay out of the Great Glen altogether, rather than along it. This meant for most people heading up the road to Errogie, which took them high above the loch, to the far side of its eastern containing ridge. To a considerable measure they were then sheltered from the ensuing catastrophe, not as sheltered as Tom and Flora, but life itself was safe. At the end of an intensely cold and miserable ordeal the way was open for them to reach safe country to the south of Inverness.

The death toll was heaviest among the military and

summer visitors who insisted in the face of obvious disaster in driving into the Great Glen, mostly from the north. The military stationed along the loch stayed at their posts, again in the face of obvious catastrophe. The major eruption began with the whole water of the loch being lifted bodily a hundred feet into the air. A thousand million tons of water fell in grotesque cascades all along the margin of the loch, drowning instantly any who had been unwise enough to remain there.

Tidal waves of enormous height raced along the Great Glen. The one that swept to the south roared and foamed through the small Loch Oich, poured in a fantastic torrent over the Laggan locks, and continued with little loss of energy through Loch Lochy. A wall of water thirty feet high crossed the seven miles of low-lying land from Gairlochy to Fort William. It poured ten feet deep into the town's long dismal main street. This was close to midnight, at which hour not many people were abroad. Most were in their homes well above the main street, and to this they owed their lives.

A similar wave crashed its way to the north covering the low lying parts of Inverness. Because the city is a comparatively open area, the low lying parts were quite extensive, so the resulting depth of water was not as great as it was for the more enclosed south-going wave. Nevertheless a goodly proportion of the people of Inverness were startled and staggered by the raging torrent that poured two or three feet deep through their homes.

The trees, the broom, the grass and the flowers that

had bordered Loch Ness were now buried by rocky debris thrown up with the water. To all appearances they were dead too. Yet within a few years they would return. Such is the irrepressible strength of the biological world.

John Stewart's reaction when he first heard of the outburst from Loch Ness was 'I told you so.' He was pleased to have been proved right. When he thought of the disaster he was appalled at his own egoism. If it had been his choice, between normality plus being wrong and catastrophe plus being right, which way would he have decided? Logically he would have plumped for normality, emotionally for catastrophe. Which just went to show what a dubious lot people who operated on emotion were—art and all that.

The Tomdoun area had become a torrid scene, with many comings and goings. The hotel there was full to overflowing. Prefabricated huts to the west, used by workers on the hydro-electric scheme, had been taken over. A radio-transmitter had been erected. This maintained full communication with the outside world after physical passage across the Great Glen had been made impossible by the floods, which now overwhelmed the road from Invergarry to Spean Bridge. Physical communication depended on a circuitous route, first by road to Kinlochourn in the west and then by small boat to Mallaig followed by a larger boat to Oban. Restricted supplies of food and fuel were already arriving at the Prime Minister's Tomdoun H.Q. by the evening of the day following the disaster. This was the time when Tom and Flora had come so close to the fireball on the ridge above Loch Ness.

Tom and Flora slept deeply that night, exhausted by the strangeness of the day. The following morning even though the rain had been stopped for some time, Tom knew the burn he had to cross would still be in flood. So the day was spent transferring food and petrol from Flora's car to the Land-Rover.

A little over thirty-six hours after the rain stopped they were on their way. There was a long run downhill for a mile through the woods. Tom used this descent to start the Land-Rover's engine. At the bottom he found a wide fairly flat place where he could drive through the still rushing stream. At Torgyle Bridge they found the stone arches, high as they were, had been entirely swept away by what must have been a truly fantastic torrent. There was now no way across the still foaming Moriston River. Thanking his luck that they were on the south side, Tom swung the Land-Rover left.

Everywhere along the road to Cluanie there were bad washouts, but these yielded without undue difficulty to the four-wheeled drive. The metal bridge at Cluanie was bent but not broken, so they were able to take the road towards Invergarry until swinging finally to the west for Tomdoun.

A military barrier blocked the road to Tomdoun. Tom got out to argue with the guard. He stood there, a stocky individual in his old pullover and inevitable woollen cap, arguing as best he knew how. But all the eloquence in the world would not serve to get him through that barrier, so he simply backed the Land-Rover off the road and settled down to wait.

The wait was a long one. Hour followed hour. Still the guard would neither let him through nor take a message. Even when the guards were changed Tom had no luck.

It wasn't until 8.30 a.m. the following morning that Tom caught sight of a fair-haired young man in civvies. Instantly he let out a great hullaballoo. Luckily it turned out to be John, otherwise Tom would have felt a bit of a fool. John tried arguing with the guards but even this was useless. Tom just didn't have the right military pass. So with a knowing gesture John walked off, to return twenty minutes later with the P.M.

Now at last the barrier was removed. Tom gave the guard a big wave as he drove his vehicle through.

'Well Mr Cochrane, we meet again,' said the P.M. as Tom pulled the Land-Rover to a halt outside the hotel.

'Apparently so, Prime Minister.'

'And what is it this time?'

'This time?'

'I've noticed our meetings always presage some disaster.'

'Then I doubt if you'll be disappointed,' growled Tom.

'How's that?'

'I'm wondering if you've been missing any planes.'

'I think you'd better come inside and explain exactly what you mean by that remark?'

Tom went into the hotel leaving Flora to see if she could locate Jeannie. They'd converted the dining-room into an ops. centre. There was a conference table surrounded by electronics: telephone, radio, TV receiver, plus acres of auxiliaries.

Tom wasn't pleased to find three officers there. After

waiting nineteen hours at the barrier he hadn't much sympathy with the military. He unbent to the extent of giving them a quick description of his experience on the ridge above Loch Ness, of the fireball with the lilac-coloured eye, and of the plane which had been so devastatingly atomized.

'It explains a lot,' nodded the Prime Minister. 'We've had reports of over twenty planes missing. No trace of any of them.'

A phone rang and one of the military picked it up. Tom had no idea who he was as everybody had been so much in a hurry to hear his story of the fireball that no names had been mentioned. The man listened then slammed the phone down.

'There's been almost total destruction at London Heathrow,' the man announced. 'Very heavy destruction of planes on the ground, the runways melted and fused, like glass, without friction. Extensive fires.'

The furious buzz of conversation which followed this unpleasant news was interrupted by a further communication. More planes destroyed, this time in mid-air on the flight paths to Heathrow. As the morning wore on further intelligence followed, always along the same lines, planes destroyed on the ground or in the air. By mid-afternoon reports of similar disasters were coming in on a world-wide basis. Milan, Geneva, Paris, St Louis, Chicago, and then Kennedy Airport totally destroyed. The list went on growing with increasing momentum. Then an apparently discrepant case of a devastating attack on Manhattan, in the region of Forty-second and Park.

'Ask them if there's a helicopter station close by,'

said Tom. But his remark was drowned in the general hubbub in the dining-room.

Tom decided to leave. Everybody seemed pre-occupied, so he simply walked out, noticed only by John who quickly followed him from the hotel.

'Why so fast?'

'I'm going to get Flora over to Kinlochourn. She'll be glad of a bath.'

'A bath?'

'Yes, I could do with one myself.'

'What the hell . . .'

'There's nothing I can do about it. Those fireballs are going to go on burning up planes until nothing is left flying. It may take days, a week, or weeks. But that's what's going to happen.'

'Well?'

'Well, there's no point in just standing around while it happens, is there?'

'Why Kinlochourn?' asked John, amazed by Tom's attitude to the situation.

'I'll be at the farm there.'

'A friend?'

'Yes.'

'What's going to happen?'

'I don't know. If anything new turns up you can pop over to see me.'

'I suppose so,' said John, irritated by Tom's composure.

'You've got to learn to relax, John. If there's nothing to be done, there's nothing to be done.'

Tom and Flora drove the twenty miles to Kinlochourn in silence. They were both tired, following the strenuous days out on the hills. Bob Frazer lived at a big farm house just as you came down the hill to Loch Hourn. In summer it was a splendid place but from November to February it was hardly touched at all by the sun. Tom wanted to think, to see if he could catch hold of ideas that were bouncing around in the back of his mind. This was why he'd deliberately come away from the scene of action in Tomdoun.

Reports of disaster continued to pour in over the next two days, as Tom had predicted, except that the concentration was now greater. The fireballs were apparently working to a concerted plan to suppress all human communication by air.

John and Jeannie came over on the afternoon of the second day. They had to wait a couple of hours for Tom who was out with Bob Frazer on the hills bringing down sheep. On Tom's return John showed him a sequence of satellite pictures which had come in the same morning. Tom shook his head 'That's very strange, isn't it?' he said, pointing to the North African coast.

'I don't know. I don't have much feeling for this sort of thing. But the met. men seem to think so too.'

'It looks like a storm beginning over the Sahara.'

After that John kept bringing satellite pictures to Kinlochourn. He would leave them with Tom, who would spend many hours studying them.

Meanwhile the air temperature became hotter and hotter with each succeeding day. It blew strongly from the east like a draught from a baking oven. The sun beat fiercely down from a cloudless sky the whole time.

Tom recalled the icy deluge on the ridge above Loch Ness. In this raging heat it seemed but a distant memory, so much is our consciousness concerned with the sensations of the immediate present. Mercifully the evenings were cooler because the air was very dry, so heat was radiated readily out into space.

The Prime Minister came over on the evening of the sixth day. Tom suggested that they go out on Loch Hourn. The outboard on Bob Frazer's boat started immediately and they were soon chugging down the arm of the loch towards Arnisdale.

Tom eventually shut off the engine. The two men sat quietly watching their surroundings.

'You don't think there's a danger of this loch going up in the air?' began the P.M.

'No, not unless the whole sea goes up.'

'What we've been trying to find out is what these fireballs are?'

'Nobody is clear about it?'

'No.'

'Well, I'm willing to speculate,' began Tom. 'That's not to say that I'm anywhere near right, you understand, sir.'

'Of course.'

'It's a new form of life, isn't it?'

'From where?'

'From space, I suppose. There's been plenty of speculation about creatures from outer space landing here on the Earth.'

'Flying saucers?'

'There's plenty of debris, such as rock, glass and so forth coming in through the atmosphere. Plenty of pieces big enough to carry information required to build a creature. The most interesting point is that we here on Earth have always seen these monsters and creatures in terms that are more or less like ourselves. That's been the extent of our imagination.'

'This is different?'

'About as different as it could be. This is a fiery creature of the air. It brooks no interference with its own chosen medium. This is why it has destroyed our man-made planes. It's simply swept them from the air as we might sweep away a few scraps of dust.'

'I haven't told you yet, but our radio transmitters are being blotted out as well.'

'I suspect you'll find anything passing through the air, material or pure radiation—anything belonging to us—will be ruthlessly destroyed.'

'Why?'

'To clear the decks.'

'For what?'

'For the battle which has now been joined.'

'Battle!'

'Yes, a true war of the worlds. A battle for the atmospheric circulation. The creature's aim is to take over the whole atmosphere of the Earth, to direct and control it. What land, or territory, is to us humans, the atmosphere is to this creature.'

'A strange idea.'

'That's the way I'm beginning to see it, after studying those satellite pictures.'

John was over with Jeannie the following morning. He had heard about Tom's idea of a 'war of the worlds' and was excited about it.

'Look!' he exclaimed, pointing at new satellite pictures. 'That storm over the desert. It's really something now.'

The storm over the Sahara had grown into an enormous cyclone of spiralling cloud. It had indeed become the most distinctive feature on the pictures.

'How d'you make out that these fireballs are alive?' asked John, after Tom had finished his preliminary study of the pictures.

'You come to the old conundrum about life don't you,' replied Tom. 'What is life? A fish obviously is alive, a stone obviously isn't. It seems easy when you put it like that because the qualitative difference between fish and stone are enormous. But if you go on arguing in this way you soon find yourself in the position of defining life as the world of living creatures, or some such nonsense.'

'I get you.'

'So I'd rather say a living creature is that which contains information, and is that which acts with purpose.'

'How about a computer?'

'Information, yes. But not much purpose about a computer.'

'When did you get this idea?'

'I suppose I had it in a vague form when I saw the portrait of Balldragon on the hotel wall. The fireball had information in it to make the portrait.'

'Where did Loch Ness come into it?'

'I think the creature had to go through a sort of chrysalis state.'

'On the bed of Loch Ness?'

'Yes, building up the enormous store of energy we

talked about. It had to do that before it could emerge.'

'I suppose the depth charging spurred it on?'

'Oh, the creature must have been ready anyway. The bombing only triggered it.'

'Any idea where it came from?'

'It could have come from any one of a million stars.'

John returned a couple of days later with more satellite pictures. The storm in the Sahara had gone. It didn't need Tom, or anybody deeply versed in meteorology, to see that the atmospheric global patterns had changed back to their usual forms.

'It's finished,' said Tom as soon as he saw them.

'The threat?'

'If you call it a threat.'

'Don't you?'

'In a way I suppose so. But I suspect this creature wanted the air, not the land or sea. I've an idea it would have left us pretty strictly alone.'

'As long as we kept out of the air.'

'That's right.'

'Why d'you say it's finished?'

'I'm pretty sure it was trying to adjust the atmosphere, particularly the winds and the general flow pattern, to suit its needs. A bit like us landing on a new planet. We'd start to grow things, to till the land, to change it to suit our needs.'

'But what was the need?'

'I suppose to recharge itself, to use the sunlight and air in a suitable way.'

John thought for a moment.

'Then really it was competing with the Sun, not with us at all.'

'You mean with the Sun driving the air circulation?'

'Right. There's tremendous energy in sunlight. This creature had a lot of energy itself by our standards but I wouldn't have thought it was nearly enough.'

'Compared to sunlight?'

'No.'

It was Tom's turn to pause.

'I can see two answers to that,' he said at length. 'Maybe it was only trying to change balances, equilibrium points. Look, the weather changes quite a bit from one year to the next, doesn't it, due to fairly small influences.'

'It could be, I suppose.'

'The second point is that Loch Ness might have been much bigger. The creature wasn't to know beforehand.'

'Bigger, with more water and more energy, you mean.'

'Yes, maybe with ten times more energy, or a hundred times if you like, this struggle to control the atmosphere would have come out the other way round. Maybe the creature would have won.'

'So you think the whole thing was for nothing?'

'It looks that way.'

The two men walked on for a while. They were by the edge of Loch Hourn. John looked down the expanse of water towards the sea. For some reason which he didn't understand he felt strangely sad.

EPILOGUE

The following morning Tom and Flora left Kinloch-ourn. At Tomdoun they stopped for a cup of coffee with John and Jeannie, and a fill up of petrol.

Tom drove back to Cluanie Bridge the way he'd come after the Loch Ness explosion. At the bridge he turned west, past Cluanie Inn and down Glen Shiel. The new road which had taken so long to build was now a mess of tar and stones. From Shiel they continued along the road to Skye, through Dornie to Ardelve. Here they turned off the main road to the north-east, along a small road which winds its way to Nonach Lodge. The heat of the previous week had dried up the flooding, so that most of the smashed roads and tracks were passable. From Nonach Lodge they continued to Killi-lan where they turned south and then west on an un-surfaced road drove to Iron Lodge.

Here they quit the Land-Rover as there was no possibility of driving past Iron Lodge. Tom shouldered his rucksack and they set off to the east.

Five miles to the east of Iron Lodge lies the head of Loch Mullardoch. Tom wanted to know if Loch Mullardoch was now a great gash in the ground, empty of water, like the monstrous trench of Loch Ness.

Consumed by a burning curiosity to know what lay ahead Tom set a great pace. The track seemed to go on for ever. Always there was another twist to it, always it seemed the next corner would give him a clear view. Eventually it did. Tom could see water. Another hundred yards and he could see the familiar head of Loch Mullardoch.

He waited for Flora to catch up and then the two of them strolled down to the lochside. Flora found a pleasant spot and settled herself to reading a book.

Tom climbed the slopes of An Riabhachan for perhaps a thousand feet. Loch Mullardoch lay below in the sunshine, just as it had done the day he and Willie Ferguson had come there by boat from the eastern end.

Tom remembered the deuterium measurements. He remembered the value for Mullardoch. It had been low, like Loch Ness. But unlike Loch Ness it had been just within the possible range for snow. So far as the deuterium was concerned, Mullardoch just could be normal. But Tom also remembered the fireball Willie Ferguson had been so unwilling to speak about. He gazed down for a long time. In his wanderings among the hills Tom had long since lost a sense of distinction between what was alive and what was not. To him the wind, the rain, the streams, the air, were all alive. He'd not been disturbed to encounter a form of life so utterly different from our popular concepts. He had no sense of worry or of horror that some new creature might still be down there in the waters below him. The thing that hit Tom, overwhelmingly, was a sense of wonderment.